Editor's Corner

It is with a bitter-sweet emotions that we greet you, dear reader.

The weeping figure on our cover tells a sad story.

You hold in your hand (or view on your e-reader) what is possibly the final issue of *Nebula Tales*, so no wonder our figure weeps.

A year ago, one man had a dream. He invited others to join in his dream and many answered the call. Writers, artists, poets and seekers of the finer pleasures joined him and embraced the tales of the Nebula.

New, exciting writers and artists were given the chance to have their work published and seen by others. For some, this was a dream come true and we at *Nebula Tales* have been, no, we *are* proud to have made some dreams come true, not just our own.

In keeping with our tradition, in this issue we feature our established authors, introduce new talent, such as

Vicki Day and showcase exciting artwork, like that of Polish artist Weronika Ślązak, whose tearful warrior adorns our cover this issue as well as illustrating the appropriately titled, *When the Last Candle Dies.*

However, as so often happens with a bold, happy band, the roads lead separate ways and each must tread their own path. And so it has happened with our merry band. Life has led some of us to new adventures where others cannot follow and our dream must be laid aside for now.

We would like to thank those who have helped us along the way, proofreading, editing, spreading the word and submitting work. Sadly, not all has been included.

Nebula Tales burned bright for a year and now… who knows? Perhaps the flame will smoulder and continue to burn or perhaps it will die and be remembered as a bold venture which brought pleasure to those happy few who embraced it.

Perhaps in the future, it will rise like a phoenix (and we have some of those in our number) and burn bright again, but for now, dear readers, we must bid you farewell and thank you for your loyalty. Maybe we shall meet again on our winding highways; may your roads be long and joyful (just watch out for the vampires, monsters and demons!).

The Nebula Tales Team.

A classic

M. Ait Ali

I stare at that blank page in my computer
from noon until stupid-o'clock
questioning my being as a writer and my being as a failure
a hopeless writer or a bogus poet as you please
dissipating my flesh and blood into a series of hours
chain-smoking two full packs and draining 6 cups of coffee
waiting for something grand, majestic and profound
to make that irritating blinking text cursor disappear for a while
what should I write about ?
Women ? I only had one in my life
what must I know about women after all ?
My failures ? To what extent may my failures interest or bore readers ?
Or the fact that I am living with just 3 dollars a day
and expecting my gibberish books to reserve me

a seat along with a big-natural-round-boobs German
girl
in a gastronomic restaurant in Paris ?
My inamorato, what will be your next poem about ?
And will you love me as Dmitri Karamazov loved
Grushenka, will you ?
She would say, And i would give her an indifferent look
then stare at the opposite of her side and say : " you
are missing the whole point,
I am Morocco's Shelley or Kafka, yes Kafka ! That
must be sufficient to me."
Or should I write about my impotency the pills give me
and when
the miracle out of the blue happens a day after several
months
and finally I get hard then masturbate to the first
imaginary lady,
oh I ought to quit lying, men don't masturbate to
imaginary women
trust me ladies, despite it may hurt your feelings,
but there is something fishy about your husbands and
their intimate fantasies...
Oh I will write another book in French that will certainly
be a CLASSIC

and I will even gather few other poets and create a
new movement in poetry,
yes something more magnificent than the beat
generation or the romantic era
and my books would be selling terrifically and then my
impotency would be cured
and I would develop a bad drinking habit and be an
addict to Absinthe too just like
Arthur Rimbaud but definitely not gay and definitely not
childish.
Oh what should I write so that all of this can come
true ?
Should I copy Stendhal or settle for the war reporter
Hemingway ?
How can I know ? I am not seeing myself shooting
myself in the head yet *but I still have a classic coming*
and both my ego and amateurism are in its way.

A country for Bullet Ants

M. Ait Ali

A country
for no one
a country
of no warriors
with iron shields
of no heroes
with fashioned caps
of no preachers
with eloquent speech
a country
where no whistles
can be heard
where no applause
can be received
a country
of domesticated Pythons
of domesticated Tarantulas
of petted Bullet Ants
gentle stings with neurotoxins
A country

for no religions

for no heavy beliefs

A country

where no one grows old.

Just age spots on wooden trees

A country

where

no one asks

what's for dinner tonight ?

Ashblood House

A.J. Touhig

Ann climbed up the old wooden staircase, feeling as if her legs weren't her own. Heavy and laboured, she recognized the faded, yellow wallpaper torn and flapping off the walls, like a dead bird flailing against the window. The bedroom door was left open, creaking, and the window was ajar, with the trace of a sea breeze on the air, salty and faintly metallic.

There was something else though that was vaguely familiar. An odour, sweet and sickly which she couldn't place. She'd been here before, the blue and yellow wallpaper, the tread on the stairs, and the room. She could hear it, feel it. The fear of what was up there in that room.

As she walked in, she felt as though everything was in slow motion. She sat down in front of the mirror, the silver hairbrush was still there on the wash stand, along with the creme, lace tablecloth and silk neckerchief. In the mirror, a vase could be seen, which lay overturned on the floor where a pile of roses lay rotting and decaying. And right in the corner to the left of her… She thought then that she was going to be sick.

As she sat forward, her gaze caught the blue and yellow flowers on the china wash bowl and she felt the bile rising with that same metallic taste again. Blue and yellow cornflowers. She remembered them, and also the room. She heard it before she saw it, the noise and deafening dread . Drawn to the door, she got up and made her way over to it, whatever it was dragging her in. It loomed over her, pressing down, the dragging noise as the teeth and metal blade closed down towards her..

"Diane! Wake up, you're going to be late!"

The voice jolted her awake, over the grating buzzing of an alarm clock. Sun streamed through the curtains making her eyes water. Feeling groggy, it took a few seconds for her to realise where she was, the dream still heavy in her mind.

"Did you have a nightmare again?" John asked.

Catching her breath, her body a ball of sweat, she gave a muted reply. She had. It was the same one, the same she'd had ever since they came there, always the same. It never varied, in fact it seemed to be getting more frequent, urgent. Ever since she'd lost the baby. Ann didn't want to worry John anymore though, especially after all they'd been through. This was supposed to be their retreat, *respite*, the doctors said. She needed rest. They both did. She was just being silly, it was the aftermath of what had happened playing on her mind. She just wished the feeling of dread would go away though..the house, it was getting to her. She couldn't seem to shake of an unfathomable fear. It was as though every nerve in her body was taut and ready to snap. Then after a while, it would dissolve and dissipate into some reasonable form of reality. She looked at John and smiled reassuringly. Bless him, it wasn't his fault, none of this was his fault.

She had liked the look of the cottage as soon as she saw it. It seemed familiar, like an old postcard, inviting somehow, as if it needed her. It had a long gulley that ran up one side and a small courtyard, with two old out houses, leading up to a long rambling garden which was covered with heavily fragranced 'Copper Albert' roses down one side, pear and plum trees in the other, a raised herb bed, greenhouse, and a coal shed at the very top. It was the very feeling of wildness she loved, untamed. It just seemed to cry out for love and attention. It reminded her.

“Stop day dreaming Ann!', Hurry up!”

Poor John, he lived for his work. He was a creature of habit, nocturnal almost. Nothing seemed to disturb him. Hurriedly washing and getting changed, she got into the car and they were gone. She had an interview that morning, looking after children. She couldn't have any so it seemed the next best thing. It was her idea, which John didn't seem to think was a good one, but she'd insisted. Kissing her quickly on the cheek, he dropped her off and was gone.

The interview didn't go well. She couldn't concentrate on the questions, and for some reason her thoughts kept going back to the house. She felt sure she'd been there before. It all seemed so real, *Country Living*, the title had said in the magazine on the coffee table with the chintz pattern and picture of roses. She could feel the sweat starting to break out on her forehead, questions, endless questions... Biting her lip she could taste the blood in her mouth. Her head was spinning, “Can I use the toilet please?” *lease, please don't be sick!*, she told herself. She had to get a grip.

Splashing water on her face, she made her excuses, and left. “We'll be in touch!” they said. She couldn't wait to get out of there.

Outside in the fresh air, she felt better. How ironic, *Get away to the countryside* the doctor had said, *You'll feel better!*

She'd never felt worse.

Don't rush things, they said, *One step at a time*.

They hadn't moved in for very long, about 3months, when she'd got to know their neighbours. The house was over 100 years old, and had been owned by a doctor and his wife and child. The child hadn't lived long apparently, cot death they said. It had then remained empty for years until after the couples death; there'd been a fire, and it had had to be completely renovated. She and John were the first couple to have christened ,the neighbour said. For some reason the choice of words left Ann feeling uneasy.

John was going to be late that day, so she made his tea early and decided to take a nap. The day had left her feeling drained, and her headaches were getting worse. Having taken her tablets, she ran a bath and poured herself a large glass of wine. She must have drifted off when the tap started to drip. It took on a monotonous sound, which seemed to echo through the bathroom and house. Drip, drip.. the sound was almost hypnotic, leaving her feeling warm and relaxed. A hazy feeling had taken over her, but still the drip drip. It was as if it followed her around, the noise filling her head. She switched the tap off, but the noise seemed to echo and began to vibrate louder from every room, until she found where it was coming from. Afraid to move, she felt riveted to the spot, but she knew she had to go up there, drip drip..and that was when she saw it. The blood seeping out from under the door onto the floorboards, at the top of the stairs in front of her. That's when she screamed. The bath overrunning, she pulled the plug, threw a towel over herself, went downstairs and got herself another drink. She downed it in one. She really had to take hold, just another nightmare she said. John would think she was losing her mind.

Splashing water over her face, she was going back up to get the towels, when she saw them, blood spots, on the stairs. Bending down, she touched one with her finger, fresh. She heard the door then, quickly, she went downstairs.

“Sorry I'm late love”, he said, kissing her on the cheek.
“You look pale, are you alright?... H did it go?”
“How did what go?” she said blankly.
“The job!, did you get it?” he asked. Struggling to answer for a minute, she felt a rush of relief.
“Oh, no, I don't think so. I'm glad really.” Fussing over his coat, she gave him his tea and poured him a glass of wine. She was relieved that he was home. Going back upstairs to clean the bathroom, she noticed the blood spots had gone.

She walked into town the next day, to buy John a nice piece of steak, his favourite. There was a local butcher’s around the corner, recommended by Joan, her neighbour.
“Morning Mrs Killmore, how's life at the at the new house suiting you?” Word had travelled fast.
“Oh, you know, nothing like a change of scenery, clean air, that sort of thing.” she replied, not really thinking what to say, as she watched him wrapping the bloody steak. He handed it to her with a smile,
“That's the ticket! Cures all evils!”
Not this one she thought. Thanking him she left.

That evening she had poached eggs on toast, she couldn't face anything else. Leaving John at the computer, she took a sleeping pill and went to bed.

Drifting off into an uneasy sleep, she awoke to the sound of something rattling, it sounded like someone running their fingers against metal. She got up and followed the sound, trying to make out what it was. Rattling?, then laughter, a baby laughing! She followed the sound to the bedroom. It was a pleasant sound, gurgling, then when she reached the bedroom door, it stopped. Something had dropped.

As she opened the door, she saw it right in front of her, a baby's rattle on the floor. She picked it up. The noise was coming from the corner of the room from what looked like a cot. But when she got closer, she realized it was a cage. Peering inside, the gurgling had stopped and turned to snarling. Something inhuman lunged out at her, screeching, latching on to her, biting her. She couldn't get her hand from out of the cage, then the blood began pumping out of her, she couldn't stop it: The noise, screaming, the metallic teeth bearing down… Screaming, she couldn't stop screaming.

Her husband got up.

“I've had enough of this Ann! For once and for all we're going to put an end to this,” he declared as he marched up the stairs to the bedroom. “Ann, for God's sake, come back down here! There's nothing up there.”It was then he saw it, *a … baby?* gurgling on something, laughing? And his wife, covered in blood, on the floor, still nursing the thing that was feeding off her, in what used to be her arms.

Car Repair Manuals

Written By: Jim Conley

BY FAX (No response received as of yet).

March 4th, 2018

Haynes Auto Repair Manuals

859 Lawrence Drive

Newbury Park, CA 91320

Attn: Technical Research Division

Please find enclosed the manuscript for my novel 'The Devil In Reverse'.

I have been reading books published by Haynes since 1987 when I made the brave decision to change the oil filter in my 1981 Toyota Celica myself. Since then I have bought and sold several hundred automobiles and consider myself a proficient mechanic and a knowledgeable collector. Your clear insightful editing and pioneering use of numbers to identify what to do next remains the industry standard for auto repair.

As the proud owner of the last road certified 1965 Citroen DS in Canada, I rely on the two volumes of Haynes Repair Manual #814 to ensure my green 'Goddess' is maintained as close to original factory specifications as possible. I have been able to have very sexy parties with up to nine people in my DS. I am a well-loved man.

As you may surmised I am passionate about all things automobile and consider myself a detective of sorts. While I know nothing about guns (nor do I have any interest in acquiring such knowledge) I am a widely respected expert in my own field of expertise and have contributions to make to literature as well.

'The Devil In Reverse' is a stylish auto maintenance thriller featuring Senior Traffic Inspector Ingrid Catalytic of INTERPOL who convinces veteran mechanic Cameron Shaft to come out of retirement.

Nine mechanics found dead in service pits across Europe - Chief Jurgen Axle needs answers now and assigns Catalytic to the case. Catalytic's intuition tells her a single killer is responsible but Forensic Vehicle Inspector Otto Pinion says the service records match the on-board codes in all nine explosions. Catalytic disagrees with Pinion's report but Axle closes the file. Piecing together evidence in her garage at home at night, Catalytic is stumped by a routine 2004 Ford Expedition tune up that turned deadly. Remembering a column Shaft once wrote for European Car & Driver on wire harness irregularities, Catalytic tracks him down in retirement at his Stuttgart bungalow.

Shaft fills his days modifying Smart cars for off-road racing and has no interest in the case until he hears his rival Pinion's name. Using his hand built ODB2 scanner, Differential discovers undocumented onboard sensor codes through his Haynes aftermarket repair guide that Pinion has missed. A subsequent oil analysis leads them the trunk of a 2017 Lamborghini Huracan filled with counterfeit spark plugs and a severed human head.

Unable to interpret the Huracan diagnostics, Shaft is forced to negotiate with mysterious parts broker Hans Flywheel and his doberman Glowplug to understand the events unfolding. Flywheel hints at the existence of a nameless cartel vying for control of the automotive parts industry. From the junkyards of Prague to the board rooms of Detroit, Catalytic and Shaft hurtle towards a road-gripping conclusion that involves adjusting brake cylinder play to manufacturer guidelines and how to remove cylinder head bolts in the proper order. 'The Devil in Reverse' is guaranteed to appeal to casual readers and factory certified technicians alike.

I appreciate that Haynes is a non-fiction publisher (although your instructions for adjusting the fuel injector pump timing on the 1994 Jetta 1.9L L4 can only work in a corner of the universe where clocks run backwards while they float into the sky) but I believe there are marketing and promotion synergies both that deserve further exploration.

I look forward to discussing this matter further with your team. I believe we have the opportunity to create a bold new form of literature which entertains while also reminding people of the importance of regular fluid changes and inspections, proper tires for the season, the etiquette and physical properties of roadways, washing and detailing techniques, the relative benefits of diesel and gasoline, why cars can't fly, the pros and cons of shooting out your windows during high speed pursuit, what really happens when you pull up at the emergency brake at sixty miles an hour, what kind of cars the extremely rich really drive, cars that are actually light enough to be moved by four average men, and why red cars are more expensive but commensurately more attractive to beautiful people you want to sleep with.

Dual Destiny

Episode Four

Minnesota Nice

Brother Warren

Sitting in the pews of the chapel, Brother Warren sought the counsel he needed when he received the message he had been waiting so long to hear. *Not much longer, My Child, the Prophet draws near, just outside town, she and her Guardian should reach you by dawn, if all goes well.* The soothing voice whispered to him, around him, through him.

"Thanks, Mel," he replied softly, getting to his feet. *Better tell the abbott it's time to prepare. We were hoping for more than twelve hours, but you get what you get and you don't throw a fit.*

Brother Warren could well remember the first time he had counsel with the current abbott, the disbelief he had seen in the man's eyes, *I'm used to that particular look though,* how the disbelief turned to wonder, with each turn of a page in Brother Warren's little scrapbook. It was a lot to swallow, Even Brother Warren was willing to admit the tale he told to each new abbott a week after they were sworn to his monastery, would be enough to shake any one's sanity to the core. The little scrapbook helped. When Brother Warren was a mere five years old, he found out the hard way, he wasn't like normal children. While climbing the largest tree on the plantation, against his master's orders, he'd fallen from one of the highest branches, hitting several large branches on the way down, snapping bone after bone, nothing but a bloody, crumpled lump on the ground by the time he was found. But, he was alive and breathing, somehow he survived. Even more miraculous, after resting a single night, he was healed, not a single broken bone, no scars, no marks on his little body to tell the story of how broken it had been no more than twelve hours ago. His master accused his mother of witchcraft, had her burned at the stake in front of the other slaves, in front of Warren. It is a smell he could still remembered. Both he and his mother knew the truth, it was not witchcraft which had healed his little body, had left him unmarked from the experience which would have killed any other, it was his father's blood running in his veins, angelic blood. Warren wasn't vain enough to believe for a second he was the second coming in any form, his father had simply fallen for his mother, but couldn't love her more than his Creator and refused to stay on the Earthly plain for her.

After watching his mother burn for his sins, Warren could take the abuse from his master no longer, and he fled into the night with the smell of his mother's burnt corpse still in his nostrils. Warren had no idea where he was going, how he was going to get there, or what he was going to do once there. He knew he was but a boy, small, defenseless, and this was probably a hopeless mission. But he had to get away, as far away as possible. So Warren ran, and he didn't look back.

Many years later, being helped along the way by faces and names lost to time, Warren found himself in a small river town calling itself Mankato. Outside the newly established town, a monastery was being built on a large hillside, people here seemed nice to folk like him, and he helped to build the monastery. Warren then sought sanctuary within its walls. After the Civil War, he devoted his life to God and has been with the walls of Mount Kato ever since. Thus, the scrapbook.

The scrapbook started with the building of the monastery, when Warren first realized what it was he was doing here in Mankato, that this place was to be his home. The first photo shows a smiling young black man in a pair of work overalls and floppy hat digging a trench which would become the road leading to the monastery. Flipping forward, the young man appears again and again, never aging, always in his twenties, soon, he is dressed in the robes of a monk, standing next to an abbot. The date and time, written in simple handwriting and signed by the abbott in the picture. Next picture; new abbott, several years have passed. And so time goes on.

If not for this scrapbook, Brother Warren would possibly have ended up in a psych ward somewhere, living out his years eternally hugging himself and bouncing off padded walls.

Thanks to Mel, Brother Warren thought, *I kept the scrapbook, stayed within these hallowed walls, and awaited my destiny. It has finally come for me, for us here, I hope we are prepared to defend her. To persuade her. To protect her. To show her the good within the world, within herself.*

*

Anna & Zane

Looking around in stunned disbelief, Anna can't quite comprehend what she is seeing. *Snow? Freaking snow? In Dallas? No freaking way!!*

Zane, Anna, are you alright? Mel's voice breaks through Anna's frantic thoughts.

Without thinking, Anna answers out loud, "Mel, I am so far from ok, what the hell just happened? Where the hell are we?"

Perhaps Zane would like to explain, maybe saying it outloud will help him make sense of it, Mel says, making no sense to Anna.

Whirling around to face Zane, Anna says impatiently, "Well, spill it."

Looking a little lost, and everywhere but at her, "It's a little hard to know where to start."

"The beginning is usually a good place."

"That's just it, after passing out there back at the station, I really could go back to the beginning of it all, and I mean it all, everything, every single damn thing on Earth. I was here when it was created. Walked it with my Creator while he explained to me what the plan was for me,what I was specifically created to do.

And you know what that was Anna? What I was created to do? My purpose in life?" Zane's voice has gone soft while talking, but the intensity in his eyes tells her he was telling the truth, Anna shakes her head, and he continues, "You, you are my purpose. I am to protect you, to teach you. To defend you at all costs. Up ahead, about two miles along this road here, is the college town of Mankato, but about half a mile from here, is a monastery, this is where we are headed. They are waiting for us there. We both have much to learn. And we have to be there by dawn. Less than six hours from now."

"Shouldn't be a problem to travel a half mile in less than six hours," Anna says, trying not to think about everything else Zane has just admitted, *too much too soon, can't handle this much information.*

You know it's all true, Anna, why deny it? You knew the moment you saw those eyes looking at you from across the station. Mel whispers in her head in a much too rational tone.

"Nothing to say about it, ok, denial, got it," Zane says, still not meeting Anna's eyes, "The reason it may take more than six hours to go only half a mile is simple, we can't take the road. By now Vincent, the one from the alley, will have contacted his 'people', and I use that term loosely, in this area and alerted them to our location. Most likely they expect us to travel by the road and will keep a watch on it. We will have to go through the woods. Not exactly a walk in the park when you consider the snow, the fact that you're already shivering, and I'm not exactly wearing cold weather friendly clothing myself."

Unsuccessfully trying to stop her teeth from chattering, Anna says, "I suggest we start moving then. Movement will hopefully create some warmth, at least that's what I'm going to tell myself."

I'll tell you where to go, guide you to the monastery, lead you away from Vincent's people, and towards Brother Warren. He knows you're coming, is waiting impatiently, has been for centuries, Mel tells them both.

"Centuries?" Anna gasps disbelievingly, "How old is this Brother Warren guy? Is he going to crumble to dust if we touch him?"

He appears no older than Zane, but was born into slavery here in the States.

"So, what is he? I can sense him, somehow, like a pull on something inside me, a tug pulling me forward, but I don't understand why," Zane says.

It's really quite simple, Zane, Brother Warren is very much like a nephew to you, he is half-angel. Only his father never cut his wings, Like you did, like Anna's mother did. But he left behind a half-breed, half human, half-angel. All angelic blood calls to itself. Brother Warren is as aware of you as you are of him.

"Then why was I never aware of Anna? Or her of me? If angelic blood flows in both of us?" Zane asks the question both him and Anna want to know the answer to.

The simple answer, Anna's demon side doesn't allow it. Just as her angelic side doesn't allow her demonic blood to call out to other demons. She is shielded from both sides of the coming war. Only you, Zane, were given any hint of what was to come. Vincent got his information the way demons normally do, in evil ways, murder, torture, but I will say this, not one who was tortured, no matter how badly, gave up Anna's name. All were true to our side. Anna, you must believe in the good of this world, the fact that people, good people have died to protect you, has to mean something.

"Yeah, it means I'm just as capable of killing, torturing, of giving into evil deeds, as your next demon. I'm not as angelic as everyone seems to think," Anna says softly, shivering from more than the cold, she can't hold the memory at bay...

*

Anna's Fifteenth Birthday

Sure, it's technically stealing, but who is going to miss a single brownie? Anna thought to herself, hoping her so-called special ability to stay under the radar would kick in and she could make it out of the supermarket with her ill-gotten treat without getting caught. *It's been a year since my mom died, on my birthday, need I remind anyone who might be listening, even though no one ever is. Seems whatever voice helping me that night was indeed in my head, cuz there is no one here anymore. I'm all alone now. It's a year later, another birthday, I'm officially fifteen and what do I have to show for it? I'm an orphan living on the streets, sleeping in shelters, never staying long enough to get the help I need, because they could find me, will find me. I'm so tired, so hungry, and I just want a little bit of something to celebrate and if I have to steal it, so be it.*

She was out the door, and in the clear. A smile began to spread across her face at the thought of the chocolate treat to come when a hand closed around her upper arm.

"Excuse me, miss," a low male voice said, "but I don't think you paid for the brownie? Correct me if I'm wrong."

Turning to the face belonging to the voice, Anna was both angry at being caught and relieved at being caught by a human. The guy was completely normal, didn't stand out in any way, and Anna was ecstatic in a way she couldn't even explain to herself. *He doesn't know this,* Anna thought to herself, *But he just made the worst decision of his life.*

"I suggest you take your hand off me," Anna said calmly, "Before you regret it."

The lines on the man's face hardened at the threat implied by her words, "Listen up, missy, don't you threaten me. You're the one stealing. I wasn't going to report you, just make you give it back, but now I can see I need to do more. You're coming to my office and we are going to have a little sit down, and I'm going to call the police, they can decide what to do with you."

"I don't think so," Anna said, looking him right in the eye, "I think you're going to let go of my arm, I think you're going to forget you ever saw me, I think you're going to go home tonight and die in your fucking sleep of a brain aneurysm. That's what I think." As she had been talking, the man's eyes had slowly glazed over, going dull and lifeless, but Anna had not been able to stop herself, as though possessed by something she couldn't define. When she was done, the man's eyes slowly came back into focus, and he realized he was holding her arm, he quickly released her, turned away, and speed-walked back to the supermarket. Anna watched him go with a feeling of dread hanging over and no appetite for chocolate.

She pulled papers out of trash cans for a couple days, hopeful she wouldn't find what she was looking for, but was not surprised when she did. An obituary, the picture was the man from the supermarket, died in his sleep from an aneurysm, left behind a wife and three young kids. *Jesus Christ, what have I done?*

*

Current Day

It's bad, Warren, she is in a dark place, it may take a lot to bring her to the light.

"We will do everything we can Mel," Brother Warren said under his breath as he stood at the edge of the woods, waiting for Zane and Anna to arrive, "We can keep her safe here, the wards will hold as long as she doesn't give in to her darker side. They will not know she is here, cannot get in as long as she doesn't let them in."

And if she does? If she gives in? Even for a second?

"We fight for her, beside her, we don't give up, we do whatever it takes, I mean, *whatever* Mel, catch my drift?"

I do, loud and clear, we are here, count to five and they will break the tree line. I need time to prepare for the "whatever" we just discussed. You know how to reach me.

"Of course, but don't take too long, old friend," Brother Warren said, , by which time he , had only to count the three before two figures stumbled out of the trees onto the brick courtyard where he was waiting behind the monastery. "Zane Custos. Anna Malum. Welcome to Mount Kato. I am Brother Warren. You are known here. You are welcome here. There is much to tell, to do, and to learn. First though, you both look frozen, come in where it is warm, food and coffee has been prepared."

*

Vincent

Rubbing his temples, Vincent repeated the question for a third time, "What do you mean, exactly, when you say you can't find them? And before you answer, please don't just say what you said the last two times, I obviously heard you then, and I don't want to hear it again, so come up with something that makes more sense to me. Or else…"

The man on the other end of the phone was quiet for a moment and then stammered out, “Well, Sir, I don’t know how else to explain it really. We were watching the road, expecting them to take it directly to the monastery. When they never showed, we started searching the surrounding woods, caught the trail a couple times, but it always went cold, or we ended up going in circles. We can’t explain it, Sir. It seems they must have had help of some kind or another, but there was only the two scents.”

Vincent let out a heavy sigh, his hands dropping from his temples, he leaned heavily on his desk, “Did I not just tell you not to say what you told me the first two times? And what do you do? Repeat yourself. Are you a fucking parrot? Only capable of repetition? Don’t answer that. I have my answer. I told you what not to say, you said it.” With a snap of his fingers, Vincent heard an odd, squishing noise come from the other end of the call, followed by the phone thumping as it hit the ground. A second later, he heard air whooshing as it was picked up, then breathing on the other end. “Good news, whoever this is, you’ve been promoted. Find the Prophet. Bring her to me. Kill anyone who stands in your way. Understood?”

A woman's voice answered him this time, "Completely, Sir."

*

At The Monastery

After a warm meal, Zane and Anna were lead to a room with a large fireplace and cozy armchairs. The walls were covered in bookshelves, between each shelf was a floor to ceiling stained glass window depicting scenes of angels fighting demons. Zane found comfort in them, Anna not so much. Turning away from them, she looked at the books on the shelves. The books were old, bound in leather and fabrics, large volumes, small, thin, thick. The letters seemed weird to her at first, but it seemed the longer she looked at a single spine, the letters became clear to her. Stranger yet, the volumes all seemed to discuss angels, demons, prophecies, end of times, and half-breeds like her and Brother Warren. *Well, more like Brother Warren than me, according to pretty much everyone, there is no one like me,* Anna thought to herself.

After a few moments had passed, a door opened and two monks entered the room, each carrying a small bundle. One approached Zane, the other Anna. Behind the monks came Brother Warren, "Please accept these clean, dry clothes in exchange for what you are wearing. You will find them more suitable for these temperatures than what you are currently wearing. Also, a room has been prepared for each of you within the monastery. Please, we ask while you are here, you remain within the grounds. They are safeguarded against demons. Demons cannot come onto the property without invitation, so," here Brother Warren glanced at Anna, "do not invite them in, and they cannot enter, understood?" Zane and Anna both nodded understanding. "Good, please follow the brothers to your rooms, know they have taken vows of silence, so if they don't exactly chat your ears off, don't be offended," Brother Warren looked at Zane and Ana as though expecting something, "That was a joke, a bad one apparently, since no one is laughing."

"Very bad, Brother Warren," said the monk in front of Anna, turning to face her, he introduced himself, hazel eyes full of warmth, "Name's Brother Adam, and we have been waiting for longer than you can imagine, Anna. Centuries of training have prepared us for the war ahead, and we have all vowed to protect you. You are safe here. Now, let's get you to your room and out of your wet clothes, how 'bout that?" Anna felt her face flush at his words, "Oh, dear," Adam stammered, "I.. that's not… vow of chastity and all that… only fifteen… wasn't going to…"

Brother Warren's warm laughter rolled through the room, catching everyone off guard. He laughed deep and long, tears rolling down his cheeks. Anna caught it next, then the as yet unnamed monk, next was Adam. Zane stood looking at them each in turn, mouth open, a look of confusion on his face. "Have you all gone mad?" he asked no one in particular.

Is the end of the world something to laugh at?

Who was Vincent talking to?

Find out next time in the next issue of

Nebula Tales

Written By Jessica Oeffler

Phoenix, perplexed

Episode 2 of the serial "The Battle Hymn of the Asbahri"

By DW Brownlaw, 8300 words, Thursday 7th November 2019.

Sensations awoke first, one after the other; memory then consciousness came online last.

Feeling: wetness - no, not just wetness: a submerged body rushing down a narrow channel, feet first; a stomach-clenching drop ending in a jarring, boneless crash; a wet body in cool air, face-down on a cold metal table; reflexive coughing and gagging; mucus rising from the lungs with a pungent...

...taste: salty and earthy, familiar, like… what?

Smell: very familiar, a cross between sweetness and cleaning fluid, like… amniotic fluid?

Sound: coughing; an alarm bell ringing; liquids splashing on the floor below and gurgling through a grating.

Light: bright and white; white blurry shapes; something slimy coating the eyes?

Memory: We are... Ilker-145? Yes, and this instance is Kirel, Lieutenant.

Consciousness: Wait. Amniotic fluid? Have we been born?

Again?

The alarm bell shut off, its absence revealing the sounds of dripping and the soothing hum of an air conditioner. Kirel relaxed. If this was a dream, it was a vivid and highly detailed one. The light was so bright, the chill from wet skin was unrelenting and... since when did a dream have flavour? No, it had to be a dream or a nightmare, didn't it? Being born again was impossible.

Kirel tried and failed to focus with uncooperative eyes; tried and failed to move a weak and floppy body; tried and failed to entertain the notion of a second birth.

A synthesised voice boomed, shattering the moment. "Welcome to the Ascendancy! Pay attention. The following briefing will be given only twice!"

Kirel's whole body jerked and their heart jumped.

This was no dream. No clone could ever forget their first assignment's loud announcement. This was a real cloning facility and Ilker-145 had just been born again. But how was that even possible?

And, more importantly: why?

The familiar voice was blaring out from somewhere beyond the foot of the table. “You are a clone and the property of the Asbahri Navy according to the provisions of subsection…”

We know. Why are we hearing this again?

“Your instance is identified as Captain Nitya Ilker-158-147....”

Kirel's mouth dropped open. Who in the thirteen pools was Captain Nitya Ilker-158? What sort of wartime cockup was this?

“... and your batch size is 1. Your personal...”

One? A batch size of one? No. We are Ilker-145. We are seven.

But even with blurry sight, it was clear no child-height clones stood around the white table, no genetically identical faces were trying to commune with Kirel. There was no assembly, no sharing, no murmurs of encouragement, no reassuring touches, no entwining of arms, and no comforting bodies cuddling close on the cold table. With no assembly, there could be no communion; the world would be a cold and empty place.

If this was what it felt like to be alone, a lifetime first for Kirel, then the universe could stuff it.
Kirel called out, but their voice whispered and rasped with phlegm, bringing on another hacking cough in a bid to clear mucus from unused vocal cords. Another attempt produced a more familiar treble voice.
"Farzana? Ellenore? Dillon? Where are we? Come to the focus. Assemble. Commune."
"Pay attention, this is Team Ilker-158's first assignment..."
Why was there no reply? Had they not heard above the pandemonium? Was Kirel's voice too weak to be heard? Surely Blyss and Amelika, having heard the team focus calling, would be the first to respond, the first to assemble and commune, eyes twinkling in their eagerness.
Ilker-145 did not assemble. Kirel was isolated from communion.
The room swayed in a nauseating manner as if the facility were afloat at sea. Pain ripped through Kirel's chest, their heart pounded against ribs and breathing laboured through a constricted throat.
Why aren't we assembling? We are not complete. This instance can't survive alone, it's not natural.

Nothing else mattered. The need for intimate communion with the other instances of the Ilker-145 group mind was a twisting knot in the stomach.

Kirel tensed flaccid and aching muscles and, with straining effort, flipped themselves over and onto their back. Knees lifted and elbows pressed down, Kirel lifted their head off the table to look around. Shaking their head and blinking to clear slimy fluids, Kirel scanned the room through still-watery vision.

Towering above the head of the table, loomed the transparent, bulbous and now empty cloning tank. Slime coating its inner surface obscured details of machinery inside. Identical white metal tables radiated away from it, ten from memory, a tall white cabinet standing at the foot of each. White chutes extended out from the central tank and ended over each table. No one stood around Kirel's table and no genetically identical instances of Ilker-145 lay on the delivery tables in sight.

The room was empty. Lonely. Kirel shivered uncontrollably.

New, unexpected sounds competed with the ongoing announcement. A door crashed open, the noise coming from behind the cloning tank, and was followed by the slapping sound of running feet, many feet, with assault claws clicking on the tiled floor. Only combat troops wore such claws, but what were they doing here?

"Failure to comply with orders is punishable according to the Naval Disciplinary…"

Looking along the table, Kirel's trembling, wet and naked body resembled a prepubescent human girl's, with its knees raised and fists clenched. This instance was a standard Ilker model, so it should have been familiar. But it was a stranger's body. A pale brown alien body.

It lacked algal symbionts.

It was not green.

A primal high-pitched scream ripped unbidden from Kirel's throat. "Nooooooooooooooooo!"

The scream cut short as strong hands slammed Kirel's shoulders back onto the table and wrenched limbs straight. Four gigantic armed marines, almost twice a clone's height, surrounded the table and held Kirel down. Large fingers squeezed and pressed into Kirel's loose flesh, and a smell of stale sweat overlaid the previous sweetness. They were breeders: big, fast and deadly, clad in battleship-gray breeches, harness, and berets. They carried assault rifles and their torsos were covered by transparent gel armour that revealed rippling green muscles. They were terrifying and over-powering but Kirel kept struggling uselessly and screamed all the more.

“Team! We need to assemble, to commune! Chhabi! Blyss! Amelika!”

“...this completes your assignment briefing. Standby. In ten seconds, I will read out the announcement for the last time.”

In sudden quietness, a man behind Kirel’s field of vision took charge and issued orders. “Keep hold of the clone. Gentle now. I’ll position the gurney...”

“Welcome to the Ascendancy!” boomed the mechanical voice again, “Listen carefully,...”

The officer shouted in competition with the announcement. “Keep her still! Clear room this side for… Oh, by the sinking depths! This is impossible…!”

What did it take for a clone to be heard against all this noise? There was nothing for it but to scream louder.

“Listen! Mistake! Wrong body! No team. We must assemble. NOW!”

The marines exchanged confused glances and shrugged at the out-of-sight officer.

A tough-looking corporal stepped into view from behind the marine who held Kirel's ankles. A scar started high on her smooth pate, emerged from under her beret and dropped straight down to the jaw, barely missing her right eye. It was a furrow of pale brown scar tissue in an otherwise dark green face. That line now bent as she screwed up her face in a look of concentration and bellowed to the unseen officer, “Pardon, sir?!”

A lieutenant, also in Asbahri combat gear but only armed with a holstered pistol, came into view and strode to the cabinet. His so-called ‘ice-breaker’ chin thrust forward aggressively as he slapped the cabinet with some force. “High priority override! Stop the announcement…!”

Why wouldn't they listen? “Not our body! This instance is Kirel, not Nitya! WHERE’S OUR TEAM!?”

“... the property of the Asbahri Navy according to the provisions...”

The corporal examined a plaque on the cabinet, above a panel of buttons and twinkling lights. Though she was standing next to the lieutenant, she still bellowed to be heard. “It’s no good, sir! It’s only a class 1!”

The lieutenant shouted back, struggling to be heard over Kirel and the announcement, “Silence this idiot box, Corporal!”, and turned towards Kirel’s table.

“... and ratified by the Joint Chiefs of Staff in the plenary session held on...”

“No off switch sir, no power cord, and these buttons don’t do squat all! Orders, sir?!”

“I don’t care how you do it! Get creative!”

“Your instance is identified as...”

“Listen! Help us! Help us!” Kirel’s arms and legs were now aching and trembling uncontrollably.

“..this is Team Ilker-158’s first assignment...”

“WHERE’S OUR TEAM!” Kirel’s back arched in a futile attempt to break free, “WE MUST ASSEMBLE!”

“You are to report to Navy Intelligence at…”

Kirel froze in mid shout, and the nearest marines frowned at the change. What had Navy Intel got to do with this? A clone born with the wrong name might just be a wartime cockup. But armed and unfriendly marines had crashed in and now Navy Intel were involved. If this were a wartime cockup, it was rapidly becoming a strange and dangerous one.

A staccato burst of thunder crashed out beyond the foot of the table, making Kirel flinch. For a seemingly-long moment, nothing happened. The white-tiled room was silent, save for the ringing in Kirel's ears and the sound of electrical sparking. The stink of spent munitions assaulted Kirel's nose, restarting the coughing. Some marines shook their heads and made wide-eyed expressions at their corporal, but their grip on Kirel did not waiver.

The marine at the head of the bed, pinning Kirel's shoulders, had the best view of what had happened. He gave a low whistle. "Fuck me, corp, you killed it."

The corporal stood near the cabinet's remains wisps of smoke curling up from both her rifle barrel and the twisted, collapsed wreckage. She turned to her officer, eyebrows raised in worry. "You said get creative, sir."

"Indeed I did, corporal. But technically... that's a straightforward case of murder."

The corporal and her marines frowned and shared worried glances.

The Lieutenant grinned. "Relax. Our orders are top priority, straight from Admiralty HQ. We stop for no one, especially not a class 1 soul. Good job Corporal, I'll take full responsibility for that. Now c'mon frogs, let's package this clone and get out of here."

The marines were here for a kidnapping? What was going on? Kirel screamed and struggled anew against strong hands. "Listen to me. It's all wrong..." The black maw of loneliness opened up and dragged Kirel into its black depths. "We can't commune! WE. NEED. OUR. TEAM!"

Kirel felt a sting in the neck and turned to see the lieutenant putting a syringe back into the utility belt on his harness.

"She got real kissy real fast, didn't she sir? Didn't know it happened to new-borns."

"Nor me, Corporal. She's an odd one alright."

Not 'she', you insulting log of… This instance is not… is not… not…

Eyelids drooped, consciousness faded and voices receded into peaceful darkness.

*****

Fire! Falling from the sky. Hitting the ground. Bursting outwards. Towards us. Sticky fire.

It's stuck to our legs and side! Can't pull it off! Hands are burning!

Fire all around! Burning! Falling! Falling...

*****

This time, consciousness returned like a gentle awakening.
Dream? Of fire? Maybe. Fading now.
Kirel's neck stung. A man wearing only white breeches and a matching cap straightened up, towering in darkness over Kirel's bed, and put something in a tray with a metallic clatter.
Tall. A breeder. Nurse? Must ask him about... about... can't remember... can't...
*****

The man was gone and the room was alight with sunshine from a high window.
Kirel was alone in a small, white-tiled room, lying on a huge bed built for a breeder. For most breeders, this would have been a mere narrow cot; for some, it would not even have been long enough. For a small clone, it was too long and too wide. Its empty expanse was vast, and that was somehow significant. There was room on the bed for many more clones. There should be more on the bed. It was unnatural for a clone to lie down without company, but who should be here? And how many?
The room was white from floor tiles to ceiling panels, even the door was painted white. The room dazzled in

the sunshine from a single window. Other than Kirel's bed, the room was empty.

Nurse? Hospital?

Breeder hospital?

A sunbeam lanced diagonally across the room to light the left wall near the bed. The door had a small observation window positioned as high as a typical clone could reach. Through it, Kirel could see someone's helmeted head and one shoulder which was clad in gel armour with a strap of dark green battle harness over it. Their neck was thick and muscular.

Guard. Why?

Can't move. Why?

Can't think. Why? What's wrong... with our… with our...

*****

Kirel's neck stung again. Someone stood at the bed's right side, another enormous breeder in white breeches and cap, but this one had vestigial breasts - so, a female breeder. Bright sunlight from behind silhouetted her enormous body and hid her features in darkness. Light and shadow spilled to the floor by the right side of Kirel's bed.

Sun's moved. Time passed. Bright... too bright... Hot... too hot... burning...

The woman's halo of light changed from white to a swirling maelstrom of yellow, orange, red and black. She burned, and the ferocious flames burst outwards with a buffeting roar filling the room. The fire was viscid, adhering to Kirel's legs, coating one side of the abdomen, eating into flesh. The next instant, all of Kirel's body was ablaze. There was scorching heat and screams, so many screams. And with a roar of disintegrating masonry, Kirel was falling. Falling. Falling...

Click!

The room was once again white, safe, and hygienic. An unobstructed sunbeam lit up the floor on the bed's right.

The woman was no longer in silhouette but stood at the foot of the bed, holding a white clipboard detached from the white foot rail. She had blue eyes and a light dusting of freckles, light brown contrasting with dark green skin, extended from the top of her head, around the face and neck, and petered out over the upper arms, shoulder blades and upper surfaces of her chest. She was looking at Kirel with a slight smile tugging at the corners of the mouth and eyes. "Do I really have to advise you that it's not sensible or healthy to look directly at the sun?"

Her white cap, perched on her freckled scalp, sported the grey insignia of a navy doctor with captain's leaves. She put a used syringe in a sterile white tray, placed the tray on a white metal trolley, and made a mark with a white pen on the white clipboard.

Kirel could see through the observation window another guard beside the door, as muscular as the first.

"W-w-wha…? W-w-why…?"

"And good afternoon to you too." The doctor replaced the clipboard's pen and squinted at the notes, "Captain -ah- Nitya? Ah - Ilker-15...158…? Tsk. This writing is terrible."

No. Wrong rank! Wrong name! Wrong cell-batch!

"Nnnnn…"

"I am Doctor Soo." She hung the clipboard on the foot rail with another click. "You may be a Captain of Navy Intelligence, but you are under my care and will follow my orders. And my first order is this: no talking, not yet; your speech will be easier soon. I know that you can hear and understand me, so just lie there while I brief you on your condition."

She moved to the bed's left side, where it was more comfortable for Kirel to look away from bright sunlight. "First: you are perfectly safe. OK? You were brought in two nights ago by a special forces recovery team and you are now in the medical suite of Admiralty HQ, one of the safest places in the world. Please relax. The enemy cannot get you in here."

The doctor lifted Kirel's left arm. "Now, this is just a quick check, I examined you thoroughly yesterday morning. There are absolutely no traces of algal symbionts in your skin, none whatsoever, which is kind of rare, but as you know your body won't accept them after birth. With no algae at all, I imagine you must get pretty hungry on occasion, so I'll arrange for some albino hi-carb food to be brought to you. But you still need sunshine, even if it can't feed you, so I prescribe some sunbathing at the earliest opportunity."

"However..." She reached out to hold Kirel's head. "These stitches across your scalp are most curious..."

Scalp? Stitches? Why?

She stroked a gentle finger in a line over Kirel's baby-smooth pate, lightly snagging over things in the skin. "They'll drop out in a few days, and they'll dissolve sooner if you get enough swim time. One thing's for sure though, that incision was never done in a field hospital. Once these are out there'll be hardly any scarring; almost invisible. Very nice. That has to be the work of a master surgeon or... or maybe a cloning tank's robo-surgeon?"

She tilted Kirel's head forward for a closer look. "Well, it certainly matches the incision for an in utero psychiotomy - ah, that's when your soul chip was inserted in the developing brain tissue. But the stitches would have dissolved weeks before your birth. So what's this incision for, I wonder?"

No idea.

"Anyway, don't answer that. The Navy would probably have to shoot us both." She laughed as she lifted and lightly massaged each of Kirel's limbs. "Checking the rest of your body, I find no sign of any injuries, past or present... although, your musculature is surprisingly weak. I can't imagine what you've been through. Whoops, there I go again. Forget I said that." She chuckled again, shaking her head.

Weak body? Weak head! Can't think.

"Nevertheless, we have followed protocol and kept you in restraint and under heavy sedation, which is why your thoughts and speech probably seem sluggish.

Don't worry, this is standard for someone diagnosed with a severe case of CIS."

Kirel frowned. What was CIS?

"Sorry, I mean Clone Isolation Syndrome. Commonly known as kissy."

Isolated? From team. What team? Who? Where?

"W-w-w-w-w…"

"I said be quiet, Captain. I order you to calm down. Good, that's better. Now, you've only been under for -ah- not quite thirty hours. Normally, we'd keep you under for another two days. But your notes say that you're on a top priority mission and must report to Navy Intel late this afternoon for a debriefing."

Navy Intel? Why? Debriefing? From what?

The doctor looked away, frowning. "Though why we are now sending weak and clumsy clones into active service is beyond my limited strategic understanding. I guess that shows how desperate the war is getting... But never mind, I'm only a doctor. What do I know?"

She paused, looking away as if watching something far off, then shook her head and let out a quick sigh.

Active service? Clones? Crazy!

"B-b-b…"

“Sh. No talking.” The doctor placed a hand on Kirel’s left shoulder, the soft gesture reassuring and calming. “Orders, remember? Just listen. A security detail will collect you later to escort you to the debriefing. In theory, we’re expecting them at sixteen hundred today, but with a war on, who knows? Now, that’s far too soon for someone in your condition, but that’s war for you, and it seems Navy Intel can override a patient’s best interests. Therefore, against my better judgement, I have changed your prescription to a lighter sedative. You should start to feel the switch-over soon.”

Good. Think soon. Need to think. To remember... what?

The doctor moved once more to the foot of the bed to read the clipboard’s medical notes.

“The heavy sedation was necessary to stop you from harming yourself during the initial shock of CIS. You’ve been having injections of -ah- Letheprine4, a reliable formulation for clones. It does two jobs: it sends your body into a sleep state and binds to a receptor on your soul chip to block recent memories. It gives you a timeout, if you like, free of nightmares so that when memory returns, the PTSD -the bad memories- are no longer fresh and sharp. May not sound much to you but, trust me, it does help a little. The effect is short-lived, so you may remember staff re-administering the injection."

Yes. In the neck. How many? How long?

She replaced the clipboard and moved back to Kirel's side.

"The sedative you are on now, Adfectine1, is a relatively new treatment for CIS. It binds to another chip receptor to dull your emotions. It will stay in your system for a long while, gradually wearing off over a week. Letheprine4 wears off quickly, so you will begin to remember everything clearly this afternoon, but the Adfectine1 should then attenuate your emotional response - I mean, your emotional pain will be reduced. I'm sorry, it's not much, but I sincerely hope this will help you deal with it because... that's all I can do for you in the time allowed."

Her blue eyes drilled into Kirel.

"Do you understand? One grunt for yes, two for no. Respond."

"Hunh."

"Good. Now, pay attention. Letheprine4 has helped you, but it's not a cure for CIS - there isn't one. You had barely thirty hours of heavy sedation, not the recommended three days, so I need to be blunt. From this moment, recovery is entirely up to you and your will to live. You can give up and die, or you can hold yourself together until you are back with your team again. It's your choice. Do you understand? Respond."

We are many, and one. Both. Communing's essential. Like having to breathe. Underwater? Take a deep breath!...

"Hunh."

The doctor leant back, studying Kirel, freckles wrinkling around her eyes, lips pursed. Was that a look of pity? It was.

"I've lost two brothers and a sister in this war, and that hurts so much. But I've read that losing a clone-mate is worse than if I'd lost an intimate twin. Some say being separated from your group mind is like losing a leg, and expecting the leg to survive. Your notes say that you're missing six clone-mates, so this will be especially hard for you."

Were seven instances? Who? Now only one. Why?

"But remember: separation is not necessarily permanent. No matter what the reason for your isolation, there is always hope. If you are strong, you can cope until you are reunited - assembled, I think you call it. Of course, if this were CGS, Clone Grief

Syndrome, I... well, I wouldn't be trying to treat you, except to... ease your passing. I'm sure you'd prefer that to retirement."

Retirement? Doesn't sound so bad...

The doctor gathered herself and continued in a more professional tone. "Now then. Your mission means that you have to forgo two days of heavy sedation, right? And that's a problem. But... you're Navy Intel, a captain no less, so I'm guessing that you're tougher than you look. So, use your Intel training and focus on one step at a time. You'll need to be able to walk soon, so I'm going to trust that resilience of yours and remove all your restraints. In any case, we need to get the circulation back into your feet so you can get to the debriefing room. Can't go shuffling into that. Lie still now."

She moved around the bed, untying previously unseen and unfelt gel straps, allowing Kirel's hands and feet to tingle unpleasantly.

"You'll be experiencing some numbness and paresthesia about now... oh, you probably call it jellyfish-stings. But that will pass soon. Lie still and doze until it's gone. When it's passed, get up slowly, and massage your hands and feet. Then you can get dressed. You will find a fresh uniform in the locker under the bed. Please, dress slowly and carefully - I'm worried about your unusual musculature. Your body seems very under-exercised, even by clone standards."

Weak? Yes. Why?

The door opened inwards as a breeder female nurse came in. "Doctor Soo? Excuse me but you're needed right away in Crash 2."

"I'm just finishing up here." The doctor rubbed her temples and her eyes grew shadowed and heavy-lidded. She sighed. "It never stops, does it? But that's war for you, as I am sure you are aware more than most people, Captain Nitya. I'll come back when the heavy sedation has worn off and I'll bring a questionnaire to assess your mental state."

She turned to go, but then approached the trolley. She picked up the tray with the used syringe and turned back to Kirel. "Someone will be back later for the trolley. Forgive me, Captain, I'll trust you somewhat, but not with sharps lying around. The trolley is empty now, just in case you were wondering. I don't think even a resourceful Intel captain like you could do much self-harm with a bed and a trolley. But please, don't prove me wrong. Swim safe."

"Sw-sw-sw-swim..."

But both doctor and nurse had left, the sound of their slapping feet receded down the corridor. The guard reached into the room and, with hardly a glance at Kirel, pulled the white door closed. The deep sound it made was no mere click; it spoke of a strong, heavy-duty latch. Or lock.

Other than the observation window the door was featureless, having no handle or latch on this side.

Hospital? Or prison?

*****

Kirel woke from a normal doze in near-darkness and stretched. Skin brushed sheets with a luxurious rustling and slight crackling sound only experienced with hospital linen. This was orders of magnitude more comfortable than the blankets of a clone dormitory. A quick check revealed that Kirel was wearing a standard hospital gown, prompting the idle question: what was the point of garments that only covered the front and sides?

Light was fading from the sky outside; it was early evening. The room was already quite dark, what little light there was came in from naked light bulbs in the corridor through the door's observation window. Yet another guard stood in the corridor to one side of the door, silent and unmoving. If there was always one guard that side of the door, perhaps there were actually two, one each side?

Judging by the sky outside, it was well into the evening, perhaps nineteen hundred or later. So much for being collected at sixteen hundred. Typical wartime cockup. It would be amazing if they even remembered to bring food before morning. Kirel's stomach rumbled in an echo of the thought.

The only sound was the quiet hum of the air conditioning issuing from a small grating in the ceiling. There was no other sound, no breathing, no rustles of nearby companions. There was no movement, no attention-grabbing flick of fingers, no progression of readable micro-expressions across familiar faces, no comforting warmth of surrounding bodies. Six names, six faces, the feel of skin, scents, sounds… Kirel reached out, to touch, to hold, but there was no one there.

Kirel was an instance separated from the Ilker-145 group mind, a team focus without a team. How could

Kirel experience anything except from the other instances? How could they interact with the world without Kirel? It was impossible.

This can't be happening.

Kirel waited for panic to resume, but everything remained calm. The room did not sway in the slightest, their heartbeat was steady and breathing came easy. So, the second sedative had already taken effect, but the lack of company remained a black void in Kirel's heart, like a jet black shadow on a sunny day. At least the shadow was no longer trying to suck Kirel in as it had before.

We need to think about something else, find something to do. Get dressed? Yes, we could be taken any moment for…

What had whats-her-name, Doctor... 'Freckles' said? Debriefing? The guards outside and a door with no handle suggested it might be less of a debriefing and more of an interrogation. And what might a clone be interrogated for?

Malfunction.

It was such a bland term for the tiniest seed of clone rebellion: clones doing things that were not sanctioned. It was a term that made a mockery of the Equal Rights for Clones bill enshrined in Asbahri law. To a clone, it was a terrifying word, where even thinking it would cause a shiver. But under this sedative, it was now possible to savour the word and think about its origin without horror.

The tale of Team Bhiraj was unknown to breeders, but clones whispered it among their kind. Was it a horror story, a conspiracy theory or a fact? No matter, the possibility of rebellion had remained a fear among breeders ever since the infamous Asteroid Miners' Riot, around 150 years ago. Ever since, the slightest sign of a clone or team's independence risked being classified as a 'malfunction', with the team being 'taken out of commission' as a result. That was another polite term overlaid with shades of horror. The tale implied this had happened to Team Bhiraj -the real one- but it did not say exactly what Team Bhiraj suffered at the hands of its inquisitors; only hinting it was appalling.

Was that why Ilker-145 could not assemble? Had the other instances been 'taken out of commission' on charges of malfunction? Was it now Kirel's turn for interrogation, having now recovered from…

No. That did not make any sense. Clones did not simply get resurrected in a cloning facility with a new name. It was not only inconceivable, it was not even a logical consequence of being charged with a serious crime.

I need to do something to take my mind off this. Yes, get dressed.

Kirel sat up in bed, their new-born body trembling with unaccustomed exertion, and reached behind to untie the hospital gown's laces. The trolley, dimly seen, was still at the foot of the bed with a tiny indicator bulb that blinked slowly.

An indicator bulb?

Of course, it had one. It was a standard-issue hospital trolley, built for both human and clone staff. That bulb was on the side of a shallow, rectangular clone-terminal mounted under the top tray.

Kirel froze.

With a terminal, we might find some answers.

They sat up on the bed and swung their legs to hang over the side nearest the trolley.

And stopped.

On the one hand, there was too much mystery: Kirel's 'resurrection', confusion over their identity, separation from Ilker-145's group mind, stitches in the scalp, being drugged and snatched by armed troops, Navy Intel's shadowy involvement, and … whether all this was connected in some manner to what happened at the warehouse …

Kirel needed answers.

On the other hand, was it worth the risk? Being caught using the terminal would be seen as a clear case of unsanctioned initiative. It was foolish for clones to demonstrate too much free will; it made breeders suspicious; they preferred clones to be predictable, loyal, … obedient. The idea of an artificial soul in a near-human body was unsettling enough, without it acting with free will. That was one reason why there were so few clones fitted with class 7 souls; that, and the scarcity of such souls.

No. It was too risky. Kirel would face a lot of questions, and some would be impossible to answer convincingly.

They sat on the edge of the bed for a long time, weighing need against risk.

How can we decide this for ourselves? We are only one instance. We need...

A movement caught Kirel's eye.

Amelika was on the bed.

"Ah!"

Kirel's involuntary twitch produced a metallic squeal from the bedsprings and their eyes welled up. It was Amelika, sitting alongside, within reach. Kirel was no longer alone, no longer a focus without a team, without a purpose.

But as quickly as they had welled up, Kirel's eyes dried again. Where had Amelika appeared from? Where were the other Ilker-145 instances? How...? Why...? Kirel's heart rate dropped to normal from its sudden peak, and their body remembered to breathe again. If emotions were a loud radio, then the sedative was turning down the volume, assertively.

Amelika had flicked a finger to claim the team's focus and was now frowning at Kirel with a look of obvious impatience, so typical of them.

As an Ilker model, Amelika was a standard 'light duties' clone: short with a child-seeming body and features, dressed in the universal clone attire of breeches and tabard woven from pale dun-colored un-dyed kelp fibre. Tabards, worn only by clones, were not just cheap-to-make practical working clothes, they also served to avoid upsetting breeder sensibilities. Breeders could not handle seeing sexually immature bodies engaged in adult activity. Both sexes of breeders could go about bare to the waist but clones were expected to cover up their immature flat-chests, cinching the tabard close to the body with laces down the sides.

The flicking of fingers signalled a wish to commune, forcing Kirel to pay attention to their face. Even this close, it was like looking into a mirror: a normal Asbahri child's head, snub-nosed, with large brown eyes set in a green-skinned hairless head. Features specific to the Ilker cell-line were marginally larger skulls and ears, thin but expressive lips, and radial flecks of green in the pupils.

And yet Amelika's face was not quite a mirror image of Kirel's. Physically, there could be no differences between genetically identical clone siblings, and yet their distinct personality was there for Kirel to read in their faces. For Amelika it was a certain twinkling of the eye; a playful, sometimes mischievous, tilt to the corners of the mouth. In many ways, and for similar reasons of character, Amelika looked exactly like Blyss but was also a recognisably distinct personality from Blyss.

But new differences existed now between Kirel's and Amelika's appearance. Team Ilker-145 was 33 years old, so Amelika's large and wide child's eyes were edged with the early signs of wrinkles and their cheeks no longer had a youthful swell. This was true for all the team's members. All, that is, except new-born, fresh-faced Kirel, who was also now an albino.

A further difference was that Amelika's cheeks were wet and their eyes were puffy from prolonged crying. Kirel gave Amelika their full focus and communion began.

Little would have been apparent to people outside the group mind. This was private communication between its members, difficult to follow by other clone teams and completely unreadable by individuals like breeders and solo clones. To such individuals, it was as magical as mind-to-mind communication, silent and fast, and yet it owed nothing to telepathy. Almost as fast as thought, Kirel and Amelika communed with the subtlest changes of expression and the tiniest of gestures.

Oh Amelika, we have missed communion so much. Why are you…?

...Crying? Seriously? You've been handling too much pain and denial without help. Emotions are what this instance is for; oh, and Blyss, I guess.

Thank you. Where is everyone? Why such a small assembly?

Stop it. There's no time for chat.

What?

You want to know if Ilker-145 thinks it is worth the risk?

Yes, we do! So get on with it.

But the assembly is too small. How will we know what to

Oh Kirel, you've been the focus for over 30 years. You know Ilker-145 right down to our eye-flecks. You know what each of us think and feel, and what we'd contribute in any situation. Right now you need this instance, the impatient one, to tell you to stop dithering and get off your butt.

But what would Farzana and …

You already know! Oh, c'mon Kirel. Ilker-145 has decided. The focus must act. Move!

As if impelled by an imagined push, Kirel slid their legs off the bed and, muscles protesting, feet slapping on tiles, tottered to the trolley and reached under the top tray to feel the underside of the clone terminal box.

Yes, a data cord was coiled underneath.

The guard still faced away. But how long would that last? If Ilker-145 was not already in trouble over the warehouse incident, being caught making unofficial use of the medical facility's network might guarantee charges. The only way to get out of sight with the trolley would be to push it against the wall, near the door. Not perfect, but maybe it would be good enough? Kirel could use it there, relatively unseen.

However, if they could push it unnoticed past the door, into the corner of the room beyond the door’s hinged side, then perhaps it might remain out of sight behind the opened door. It was worth trying.

Kirel released the brake and, with legs and back trembling with exertion, steered for the corner. The observation window, as they passed it, revealed a second guard on the other side of the door, but Kirel’s sedated heart did not jump, nor did their breath catch. Kirel slid down the tiled wall to sit on the floor, pulled out the data cord, and looked back to the bed for Amelika’s approval.

It was empty.

Kirel looked at the disturbed sheets with a heart as empty as the bed. In that brief exchange, there had been no time to touch. It had been so long without physical intimacy, just one touch with one instance would have been a comfort.

If touching had even been physically possible.

Had Amelika reached out from somewhere far away?

Had they actually been on the bed at all, or was this the first sign of Kirel’s breakdown, of CIS-induced delusion?

It was possible. Amelika had not reacted to, nor even mentioned Kirels’ youthful and albino body.

But did it matter?

Whether the group mind still existed or whether it was now only a figment of Kirel’s imagination, Ilker-145’s assessment was correct, and Kirel had to act.

Taking a deep breath and blowing it out again, Kirel extended the data cord and plugged it into the socket in the nape of their neck. After a moment, they ‘heard’ the standard official greeting, as if it were someone else’s thoughts in their head.

Outward, the Ascendancy!

Please state your request.

>>>

The first thing was to establish whether the terminal would accept commands from clones other than medical staff.

>>> Report your status.

I am ready for your commands.

Warning: my battery power is at 3%, with an estimated 37 minutes of charge remaining.

Please state your request.

>>>

That explained the blinking light. If the battery ran down and the power stopped, the terminal's soul chip would die. There was no essential difference between the box and Kirel: one was a box of electronics driven by a low-class soul chip and the other was a meat machine driven by a class 7 soul chip inserted deep into its organic brain, yet both would die without constant power. And dead soul chips could not be rebooted; well, they could, but a different soul would manifest, a fresh soul with no memory. Whatever a chip-keyed soul was, wherever it resided, wherever it was summoned from when the chip was first powered up, it died when the power went off.

Death was permanent for a chip-keyed soul, just like it was for breeders with their organically keyed souls.

Kirel found a nearby power socket and connected the terminal's charger.

Status update: charging will be completed in 10 hours and 28 minutes.

Please state your request.

>>>

That was as close as a low-class soul would ever get to “Thank you”, so there was no point replying “You’re welcome”, though the temptation was there.

>>> Request access to the CAA network and open a session.

Please confirm you mean Central Ascendency Administration.

>>> Yes, we do.

Connecting.

Please state your identity or authorisation.

>>> We are Ilker-145-143205, instance Kirel, rank Lieutenant.

Connected successfully. You have 29 minutes and 56 seconds remaining in this session.

The network admin soul recognises you as a superuser on this network. Do you want to sign in with superuser rights?

>>> No, thank you. Access the Clone Personnel database with standard privileges.

Accessing.

Please wait while the database admin’s soul verifies your soul chip serial number for security clearance.

Verification is successful. You are signed in with read access. Please state your request.

>>> Access the personnel file for Ilker-145.

Access granted. Please state your request.

>>> Summarise the team's current status.

Warning: some details have been redacted for reasons of security.

Clone batch Ilker-145, full designation Ilker-145-143205, is on secondment from Central Ascendency Administration to xxxx xxxxxxxx xxxxxxxx. Objective: xx xxxxxxxxxxx xxx xxxxxxxxxxx xx …

Nothing had changed here.

>>> Yes, we know! Abort!

Summary cancelled. Please state your request.

>>> Read to me the status entries made in the last week.

There are none available in this range. Please state your request.

>>> Read to me the status entries made in the last four weeks.

There are none available in this range. Please state your request.

>>>

How long ago had the attack happened? Why did Kirel have no memory of the intervening time?

>>> Find the last two status entries.

Accessing. Two records found. Please state your request.

>>> Read the oldest found entry to me.

On 1464/04/22, Ilker-145 was the victim of an enemy firebombing attack on Warehouse 47-CJ-4521 in the abandoned Northern Facilities District of Homeland Capital. The warehouse, on the edge of the now derelict Spaceport-3, was demolished in the attack and part of the floor collapsed into the basement.

Emergency Service clones combed the wreckage and retrieved a single casualty from the basement, unconscious and with multiple fractures, crush injuries and severe burns. The casualty remained in a coma and was later identified from medical and dental records as Lieutenant Kirel...

So, this instance was in a coma? Correction - this instance's old body had been in a coma, not this new one. But for how long? And how and why had the switch of bodies occurred? Also who...

...can be found in Emergency Service report 14640422-ES-EZT-011645.

Please state your request.

>>>

Wait. What? There was only one casualty? What about the others? Did that mean…?

No. Doctor ‘Freckles’ talked about isolation, not grief. The Emergency Services report must have been wrong. Yes, Ilker-145 still lived, it was only divided. That had to be it.

It had to be.

Except, ES had a high reputation for accuracy. Its reports had to be reliable: statistics drawn from them gave High Command a picture of how the Ascendency was losing the war, bombing by bombing, incursion by incursion. Their reliability was well-known throughout Central Admin.

But the report contained no mention of anyone else found there, no other casualties, no bodies...

It was important to think about something else. Nothing further would be gained by reading the full ES report, and it probably wasn’t worth the risk spending time trawling through it. Someone might come in through the door at any time.

>>> Read the newest found entry to me.

On 1465/07/12, Navy Intelligence commenced an investigation into the activities of Ilker-145 leading up to the attack. However, with Lieutenant Kirel still in a coma for over a year, the investigation was suspended. Interim findings are recorded in Navy Intel report 14650903-NI-TDQ-566392.

Please state your request.

>>>

There was Navy Intel cropping up yet again. Why were they involved? And why over a year after the attack? Even if Ilker-145 was suspected of malfunction, that crime was outside Navy Intel's mission. It would have been investigated by the Military Police, and they were not mentioned at all. It did not make sense.

And now, Navy Intel wanted to 'debrief' Kirel, or Captain Nitya, one or the other, but about what? Maybe there might be a clue about that here? It was worth a quick peek.

>>> Follow the link to the Navy Intel report and read its abstract to me.

Please wait for connection to the Navy Intel file server.

Connected. Please wait while the file server admin soul verifies your soul chip serial number for security clearance.

Request denied. You have an insufficient security rating.

The connection to the Navy Intel file server has been dropped for reasons of security.

Please state your request.

>>>

A dead end. With only basic access rights, there was no getting round Navy security, and Kirel did not have superuser rights on that system. It had been worth a try, but what now? Kirel stared off into the darkest reaches of the room with all the energy of a children's play pool that had baked dry in the sun: empty and lifeless.

Knock!

Kirel convulsed, hands braced against the wall, ready to rise. Was someone about to come in? Would there be time to get back to bed? Probably not; breeders moved fast and Kirel’s new body was weaker than most clones’. From this angle, it was impossible to see through the observation window. Was a guard looking in, wondering where the clone had gone? It was too late to start running back to bed now and useless to stay behind the door, this was no hiding place, and it was dangerous to be found using the terminal.

Knock!

It was not so much a knock, more a bump, and it came from the lowest part of the door near the floor. Other vague sounds filtered through and around the door: muffled voices and the soft whirring of a machine. Of course. Cleaners, clones probably, working along the corridor with -almost certainly- a floor polishing machine. The Asbahri Navy loved polished floors; perhaps the Army and the new Space Corps did too. The voices were those of the guards teasing or abusing the clones; only the clone team focus might have made any reply, keeping the team safe.

The sounds slowly dwindled as the cleaners cleared this door and progressed down the corridor.

Kirel relaxed and took stock. Their stomach was empty and grumbling, but there was no sweat trickling down from a wet pate, the pulse was steady and so was the breathing. This sedative was doing what it promised on the label.

There was one more thing to try on the terminal, then it would be time to get dressed. Besides which, Kirel wore only a hospital gown and the wall and floor tiles were chilly against bare back and buttocks.

>>> Report the current status of every instance of Ilker-145.
Clone batch Ilker-145 has seven instances. A current status summary for each instance follows:
Kirel (focus): Hospitalised. In a coma for seven years, six months, 4 days and counting.
The hospitalised part was true, but not the coma, not anymore. This instance had a new body, which was strange, but why was the record out of date?
An investigation into possible malfunction by Lieutenant Kirel is delayed, pending the subject's recovery.
And there it was in the official record: that word 'malfunction'. The Ascendency was poised to take Ilker-145 'out of…'
Farzana (vault): Otiose for seven years, six months, 4 days and counting.
Ellenore (source): Otiose for seven years, six months, 4 days and counting.
Dillon (designer): Otiose for seven years, six months, 4 days and counting.
Chhabi (evaluator): Otiose for seven years, six months, 4 days and counting.

Blyss (gatherer, emoter): Otiose for seven years, six months, 4 days and counting.
Amelika (implementer, emoter): Otiose for seven years, six months, 4 days and counting.
Please state your request.
>>>
Otiose? This could not be happening. Virtually the entire group mind of Ilker-145 was otiose?
Such innocent words, ‘malfunction’ and ‘otiose’, which in other circumstances would be horrifying, paralysing even. But with the sedative, it was possible to think about their implications.
‘Malfunction’ implied Ilker-145’s cobbled-together network and computer had been found in the warehouse ruins, and so Kirel faced whatever fate had befallen Team Bhiraj.
‘Otiose’ was the term used when there was no news about a clone’s service to the Ascendency. But it was not only used to record a case of 'no information'. It also covered situations like 'unoccupied', 'missing', or 'dead'. That was typical of breeders, caring so little about clones that they would simply replace an otiose team and not bother to honour it with the reason.

However, it was not possible to become angry at discrimination and injustice, not right now. The need to be angry was there, certainly, just not the ability.

So, were the other instances dead; killed in the attack? No. If that were true, Kirel would know it, would feel it. Somehow. No, they could not be dead. They couldn't be. They were alive. They had to be.

They had to be.

How could Kirel live as a solo clone? Without communion?

Captain Nitya, whoever they were, may have been logged officially as an individual, but Kirel was an instance of a team, a small part of a group mind. How could Kirel remember and apply knowledge without Farzana? How was it possible to return to software research without Ellenore's ideas and inspirations, without Dillon's algorithms, without Chhabi's analytical skills? How would Kirel process emotions without Blyss and Amelika? Despite the sedative, the concept was unbearable. Doctor 'Freckles' was right about one thing, it would be worse than losing a twin. It would be like losing a vital organ - perhaps the liver. If the other instances were dead, Kirel could not function without them and was as good as dead already.

Kirel pulled out the data cord from behind their head. It swung against the trolley with a clatter then withdrew as a spring coiled it up.

Time passed and the tiled floor got colder on bare skin. Kirel stared out into darkness once more, seeing little, feeling nothing. Eyes and cheeks remained dry, but only because crying was precluded. The time for weeping would come days later when this sedative wore off. And then there would be more than just tears. Much more, if the other instances were… were… There would be an ending."

*****

I can always

Rewrite this

Things they try

To call to life

It rises, whatever

Prove me. Don't?

It's just your crutch

Butchered as I am

Ringing belles deep

Opened is not

Nearly enough to see

The

"Beautality"

by: Donnie Disruptor

John Oates Is Alive And Well

Written By: Jim Conley

To: editor@deeptrax.se

From: james.patrick.conley@gmail.com (Jim Conley)

Date: 9:25 AM 02-16-18

Subject: John Oates Article

BY E-MAIL

Barry Pfizer

DEEP Tracks Magazine

Suite 1200 - 632 NE 16th St

New York, New York

10956

STORY PITCH: In Memoriam - John Oates

Dear Mr. Pfizer,

I'm a freelance writer with twenty years experience (I've published thirty articles in the past year alone) and I am also a founding editor of the Swedish percussion magazine "Dunke Karrang'.

I would like to propose a one thousand word article on the death of John Oates that combines the knowledge and respect of a fan with the skills of a professional writer.

I look forward to your response and hope I am able to contribute to your magazine.

Jim Conley

Ps- I've been a dedicated DEEP Trax reader for nearly thirty-five years and your work is one of the things that inspired me to pursue a career in rock journalism. I first read Your Go-Gos road diary 'We Got The Beast' in 1982 and I've read it countless times since. I completely agree with your take on the last performance of the tour - the Ann Arbor police violated Belinda's civil rights when they strip-searched her on stage and they should have waited until the encore was over.

To: Jim Conley

From: editor@deeptrax.se (Barry Pfizer)

Date: 12:16 PM 02-16-18

Subject: Re: John Oates Article

Jim,

Sorry to hear about John Oates. I met him and Daryl back in '79. Mick was throwing a yacht party up off Martha's Vineyard. I was rubbing coconut oil into Carly

Simon when Hall and Oates pulled up on a jet-ski. Keith had a guitar and it turned into a midnight jam session with Henry Kissinger playing the spoons. Good times.

John was a good guy. He'll be missed.

I don't usually run freelance stuff but your pitch reminded me of some good times. I'll give you $500 for 1000 words but I need it back by Friday if we're going to get it into the May issue. In the meantime can you put together a quick obit (100 words?) for the web site tomorrow?

Cheers,

Barry P.

To: Barry Pfizer

From: Jim Conley

Date: 1:45 PM 02-16-18

Subject: John Oates Bio

Barry,

Thanks for the opportunity. Hall and Oates was my favorite band in high school and I still listen to them every day. I saw them 26 times over the years and I had the 'Private Eyes' album cover tattooed on my left calf when I got out of the Marines.

Thanks again,

Jim

JOHN WILLIAM OATES (1921 - 2018), missing since February 27th, 2018 and presumed dead, was last seen snorkeling near his Aruba compound.

As a member of pop duo 'Hall & Oates', Oates co-wrote over fifty top-ten hits with partner Daryl Hall during their eight year partnership. Often described as the godfather of grunge, Oates' made equally important contributions to new country and old jazz throughout his career.

As a United Nations observer Oates passionately documented human rights violations throughout Nicaragua and Laos, an experience that would inspire him to write the 1981 hit single 'I Can't Go For That'. His later efforts to standardize traffic signals in the developing nations he visited earned him the nickname 'Octagon John'.

John was a passionate hobby farmer in what little free time he had. His free range llama herd was at one point the largest in North America and he was a passionate grower of purebred oranges. In 2010 he received the Presidential Medal of Freedom for his guitar work on the 1976 hit 'Sara Smile'.

Married four times to six women, he leaves behind seventeen children.

To: Jim Conley
From: Barry Pfizer
Date: 2:10 PM 02-16-18
Subject: Nice bio

Thanks for the fast turnaround. Wow. He was a real Renaissance guy. Wish I'd known him better. Always wondered what 'I Can't Go For That' was about.

Oates only went missing yesterday? An obit might be a little premature. How did you hear out about this?

Cheers,

Barry P.

To: Barry Pfizer
From: Jim Conley
Date: 2:14 PM 02-16-18
Subject: Inside source

Barry,

I'm the Past President (Northwest chapter) of the Hall & Oates fan club. I hear things.

One of Oates groundskeepers messaged me from Aruba a few hours ago with the news. His official status is 'missing' but his snorkel and goggles came in with the tide this morning. He's gone.

There might be a body left if the sharks and the jellyfish don't get him but we're probably going to end up with another Holloway situation here. It'll be years before they officially declare him dead. He's gone. He was a crazy thrill-seeking danger junkie who rolled the snorkel dice and drowned.

Jim

To: Jim Conley

From: Barry Pfizer

Date: 2:26 PM 02-16-18

Subject: Who needs a body when you've got a snorkel?

Jim,

I get it. We've got enough to run with here. Solid source and shaky cops. Seen it a hundred times. Things are different in the Caribbean. I'm trying to remember which island it was where Stevie Winwood got himself into that trouble back in '77. Polo tournament in St, Kitts, I think. Jackie O had to fly down with fifty grand to buy off this one-eyed voodoo priest who turned out to be Scratch Perry's cousin. Good times.

There's still nothing on the newswire about Oates. We've got an exclusive and that means we're going feature. I'll give you two grand for three thousand words, same deadline.

A couple questions from the bio.

Was Oates really ninety-seven when he died? He looked good. I don't remember him being that much older than me.

He was married four times to six wives? Am I missing something? Polygamy?

Fortified compound? Tell me more. Are we talking about barricades and turrets? Sounds like a photo op to me.

Get back to me when you have time.

Cheers,

Barry P.

To: Barry Pfizer

From: Jim Conley

Date: 2:45 PM 02-16-18

Subject: Re: Bio questions.

Oates took very good care of his skin. There are rumors that he was into voodoo and bathed in goat blood nightly but we want to muddy things up with hearsay and half-truths. Leave that for the tabloids.

Most of Oates' marriages (and at least two of his divorces) took place at sea so the numbers don't necessarily add up.

Oates' compound in Aruba made Gitmo look like Barbie's Caribbean Playhouse. I've attached two photos that your art people should be able to build something from.

Very excited to hear about the feature. This is a story that deserves to be told.

Jim

To: Jim Conley

From: Barry Pfizer

Date: 7:04 PM 02-16-18

Subject: Bird is in the air.

Jim,

Bio posts at midnight. Our web editor, Raoul, did a nice job of it.

I'm confused about the photos you sent. One looks like the hut from 'Gilligan's Island' and I'm pretty sure the other is the Marine base from 'Avatar'. Was that intentional? For the time being I went with a stock Getty image of Hall & Oates.

Cheers,

Barry P.

To: Barry Pfizer

From: Jim Conley

Date: 9:15 PM 02-16-18

Subject: Invoice

Barry,

I've attached my invoice to DEEP Trax for the John Oates article. $2000 as discussed. Your swift attention to this is appreciated.

Jim

To: Jim Conley

From: Barry Pfizer

Date: 10:04 PM 02-16-18

Subject: Re: Invoice

Jim,

Thanks for the invoice. We process first Wednesday of the month so I'll make sure this gets downstairs once the article's wrapped. You'll probably see your check before the issue hits the stands. We take care of writers around here. There was this time Norman Mailer came in with a baseball bat looking for his money. Took out three windows before he remembered the article was for Lester Bangs over at CREEM. Good times.

Cheers,

Barry P.

To: Barry Pfizer

From: Jim Conley

Date: 11:26 PM 02-16-18

Subject: Re: Re: Invoice

Barry,

This is highly unusual.

Normally, I get paid before writing the article. You might decide not to pay me and then we'd end up in court for fifteen years. We don't want that, do we?

Please advise.

Jim

Ps - PayPal works best but I also do Bitcoin if that's easier.

From: Barry Pfizer

To: Jim Conley

Date: 11:30 PM 02-16-18

Subject: Re: Re: Re: Invoice

Jim,

I get it. I know what it's like being a writer waiting for a check.

I called Carol in Accounting at home. She says we don't do Paypal or Bitcoin (what is that?). I told her to overnight you the check when she gets in tomorrow.

Cheers,

Barry P.

To: Barry Pfizer

From: Jim Conley

Date: 11:44 PM 02-16-18

Subject: Re: Re: Re: Re: Invoice

I suppose that's going to have to work. You strike me as a man of your word. If you're willing to vouch for Carol then I'll make an exception this time.

I'll start working on the article tomorrow after my Commando Zumba class.

Jim

To: Jim Conley

From: Barry Pfizer

Date: 8:01 AM 02-13-18

Subject: Oates Bio - Web Traffic

Hey Jim,

Raoul just texted me. He says he's never seen this sort of traffic on a Tuesday. There's something like 200 posts about the obit in less than eight hours. I had no idea Hall & Oates still had this kind of fan base. I was listening to 'Private Eyes' on the way in. Sounds as good as it did in '81. We might have a cover story here.

Cheers,

Barry P.

Ps - what the hell is Zumba?

To: Jim Conley

From: Barry Pfizer

Date: 8:26 AM 02-13-18

Subject: Oates Bio - Web Feedback

Jim,

Raoul just checked out some of the posts on the Oates bio and it sounds like there may be a couple typos.

Can you give me a ring when you have time?

Cheers,

Barry P.

To: Jim Conley

From: Barry Pfizer

Date: 8:45 AM 02-13-18

Subject: Oates Bio - Fact Check

Jim, haven't heard back from you so I asked Brad to hold off on the review roundup and give the bio a once over. Sounds like this is going big. Apparently we're a trending on Facebook (what does that even mean?) and the website is getting six thousand hits a minute. I haven't seen this sort of excitement since Morrison whipped his dick out in Miami. That guy was endowed like the Guggenheim and he'd show it to anyone. The morning after the "Strange Days' release party we were down at Venice Beach when we saw these two nuns. I bet Jimmy twenty bucks he wouldn't whip it out in front of them. I lost. Best twenty dollars I ever spent. Good times.

Cheers,

Barry P.

To: Jim Conley

From: Barry Pfizer

Date: 9:17 AM 02-13-18

Subject: WHAT THE FUCK?

Jim,

Brad just brought me a list of screw-ups in the bio. In less than ten minutes he found thirteen mistakes. Thirteen mistakes in 150 words? A blind monkey with the clap can do better than that. Llamas? Oranges? The United Nations? The only thing you got right was his middle name.

I told Raoul to spike it but I've got phones are ringing off the hook around here. I've got VH1 on hold and USA Today is looking for our source.

Do you have any idea what you just did? Did Jann Wenner put you up to this?

Barry P.

To: Barry Pfizer

From: Jim Conley

Date: 9:40 AM 02-13-18

Subject: John Oates (1911 - 2018)

Barry,

My apologies for the delay getting back to you.

Commando Zumba always demands my full attention.

Sorry to hear there's some people kicking back at the bio. There are always going to be differences in opinion with investigative journalism.

I've started on the cover story and you're absolutely right - The compound is the hook that's going to bring the readers in. I've got a bag packed and can be on the next flight to Aruba out of Portland. Is this something I should talk with Carol about directly?

Jim

Ps - Zumba is a South American fitness program. It's like Jazzercise with maracas. It leaves me feeling godlike and fresh.

To: Jim Conley

From: Barry Pfizer

Date: 11:30 AM 02-13-18

Subject: Obituaries are not investigative journalism.

Jim,

Trust me. You are not going to Aruba.

I let Zappa interview Billy Graham. I sent the Plaster Casters to the Vatican. I let Woody Allen babysit my kids. Never, In forty-eight years of managing DEEP Trax Magazine, have I seen something go this pear-shaped. This fast.

Barry

From: Jim Conley

To: Barry Pfizer

Date: 11:45 AM 02-13-18

Subject: Teamwork and Support

Barry,

I'm a little worried here. It's starting to sound like you trust public opinion more than me. My job as an investigative journalist is to search for the truth. You as my editor have a responsibility to back me up. What would have happened if Ben Bradlee had thrown Woodward and Bernstein to the wolves like this? This isn't what they teach in journalism school.

Jim

From: Barry Pfizer

To: Jim Conley

Date: 11:52 AM 02-13-18

Subject: J School?

Jim,

I never went to J School. I learned how to report a story the old-fashioned way from guys like Ed Murrow and Walter Winchell and I made sure I got it right before I turned it in. Did you seriously go to a J School? I find very that hard to believe.

I want to see your publication list too. I just googled you and you're the Invisible Man.

Barry P.

To: Barry Pfizer

From: Jim Conley

Date: 12:01 PM 02-13-18

Subject: Qualifications

Barry,

You're right. I didn't go to journalism school. I come from a poor family of cotton sharecroppers in Oregon and had to leave school in the ninth grade to support Momma when Daddy didn't come home one winter. I learned reporting on the Internet. Perez Hilton and Matt Drudge taught me everything I know.

Most of my recent work has been Amazon product reviews. My work on the Instant Pot DUO MINI last year received a 4.6 out of 5 rating. Last month I interviewed the Zildjian 24K Light Ride cymbal for 'Dunke Kerrang'. When the translations are back I'll forward you a copy in English.

I am also a regular contributor to Facebook, Adult Friend Finder and Pinterest.

Jim

Ps - How does one become an editor-at-large for DEEP Trax?

To: Jim Conley

From: Barry Pfizer

Date: 12:30 PM 02-13-18

Subject: Re: Qualifications

Jim,

Cotton doesn't grow in Oregon.

The ratings on Amazon are for the product, not the review.

I have never heard of 'Dunke Kerrang' and you cannot interview a piece of copper. I'm going to bang your head like a cowbell if I ever see you face to face.

Are you messed up on something? I've seen most of the Rock and Roll Hall of Fame lit up and I've never seen anything like this.

Editor-at-large? I wouldn't let you sign for a pizza around here.

Barry P.

To: Barry Pfizer

From: Jim Conley

Date: 3:45 PM 02-13-18

Subject: Re: Invoice

Barry,

Sorry for the delay. More Commando Zumba. I'm just plain tingling. Did you have a chance to talk to accounting about my invoice for the feature? I'm prepared to knock 10% off the total if the money's sent out today.

Jim Conley

Editor-at-Large

DEEP Trax Magazine

From: Barry Pfizer

To: Jim Conley

Date: 1:46 PM 02-13-18

Subject: He's not dead, you don't work here!

Jim,

In the spring of 1973 Hunter S Thompson broke into my office and set my desk on fire because he thought the spirit of John Philip Sousa was inside my typewriter screaming for justice. The next morning he showed up with a new desk and a better door lock. Most importantly, He apologized.

You're not half the man he was and I don't expect any apologies for the chaos you created here. It doesn't sound like your style. You're welcome to call me and prove me wrong. My office number is 212-567-4600.

Barry P.

Ps - You're not that clever and this isn't very funny. Hunter would have shown up at Oates place in a hearse.

From: Jim Conley

To: Barry Pfizer

Date: 1:46 PM 02-13-18

Subject: My disability

Barry,

Sorry about that the signature. I've updated it.

It's probably better if we communicate by e-mail for the time being. I'm not much of a conversationalist at the best of times because of my disability. While organizing Kerrangfest XXVI last August I lost most of my tongue when I was hit in the face by an untethered gamelan. For the most part I've recovered but vowels remain a challenge.

I think we need to calm down and let things settle for a few days. For all we know he might have died in the last twenty-four hours. Wouldn't that make for a great Twilight Zone ending?

Jim Conley

Indentured Unpaid Peon

DEEP Trax Magazine

To: Jim Conley

From: Barry Pfizer

Date: 3:16 PM 02-13-18

Subject: I just got off the phone with John Oates' attorney.

Jim,

A lady named Ingrid Troutman just called me from Denver. She represents the Oates family and John is definitely alive and well at his home in Woody Creek, Colorado. He is also very angry.

He is neither ninety-seven nor dead. He has never been to Aruba nor is he a fan of snorkeling. He has only been married twice and nobody has ever called him 'Octagon John'.

I could go on but I think I've made my point. I haven't felt this used since Johnny Rotten took a crap on my desk during the Pistols first American tour.

I am explicitly telling you not to represent yourself as an employee of DEEP Trax Magazine.

Go get the help you need.

Barry P.

To: Barry Pfizer

From: Jim Conley

Date: 4:17 PM 02-13-18

Subject: I'm confused.

Barry,

If John Oates is in Colorado, who's in my basement?

Jim Conley

CEO

DEEP Trax Magazine

To: Jim Conley

From: Barry Pfizer

Date: 4:17 PM 02-13-18

Subject: Basement?

Jim,

What are you talking about?

Barry

Ps - I said cut it out with the signatures. John Oates isn't the only one with lawyers.

To: Barry Pfizer

From: Jim Conley

Date: 4:17 PM 02-13-18

Subject: I have to be honest with you.

From the law offices of Jim Conley

Re: Conley v. Pfizer

WITH PREJUDICE

Barry,

I kidnapped John Oates six weeks ago and I've had him tied up in my basement ever since. He's currently in the dryer with a load of towels.

Drowning in Aruba seemed like a good explanation for his disappearance and DEEP Trax has always been my preferred magazine when it comes to music news. It seemed like a good fit.

I suppose I overdid it a bit with the bio but Oates' real life doesn't make for good reading. He's a down-to-earth guy who plays in a popular band. The bio needed something so I added a few things to spice things up. My apologies for not mentioning all this sooner.

Jim Conley

Director of Human Resources

DEEP Trax Magazine

Ps - What is the status of the feature?

To: Jim Conley

From: Barry Pfizer

Date: 4:17 PM 02-13-18

Subject: So you just made it all up?

Jim,

Wow. You're insane. You are the strangest dude I have ever encountered and I spent six weeks on the road with Ken Kesey.

Nothing short of a picture of John Oates in your dryer would convince me that John Oates is in your dryer.

Leave me alone. I've got angina.

Barry P.

To: Barry Pfizer

From: Jim Conley

Date: 6:19 PM 02-13-18

Subject: Photo (Today)

Barry,

Please find attached photographic evidence that John Oates is in my dryer. If you look carefully you can see him nestled in the terrycloth. You'll notice the newspaper on top has today's date on it.

Ps - You'll find that Commando Zumba does wonders for your cardio. Can't recommend it enough. Ive got some drop-in coupons if you're interested.

Jim Conley

Senior Sous Chef

DEEP Trax Magazine

To: Jim Conley

From: Barry Pfizer

Date: 6:19 PM 02-13-18

Subject: Re: Photo (Today)

Jim,

John Oates is not in your dryer.

This is a picture of a dryer with the album cover of 'Hall & Oates Greatest Hits' taped inside the door window. John isn't even in the picture.

Are you pulling some sort of performance art stunt here? Andy Warhol sent me two hundred pounds of hand cream that time I said 'Metal Machine Music' was just Lou Reed jerking off with a guitar.

That was funny. This isn't.

Barry P.

Ps - I'm serious about the signature.

To: Barry Pfizer

From: Jim Conley

Date: 6:19 PM 02-13-18

Subject: Incontrovertible Photo Evidence

Barry,

I'm not sure what you're looking at but the photo I just sent you is clearly John Oates. Even without your glasses you should be able to tell by the blond mullet and blue eyes. Who else would it be?

Jim Conley

Dental Assistant Trainee

DEEP Trax Magazine

To: Jim Conley

From: Barry Pfizer

Date: 6:19 PM 02-13-18

Subject: That's a picture of Daryl Hall.

Jim,

You do realize Oates is the one with the mustache, right?

Barry P.

To: Barry Pfizer

From: Jim Conley

Date: 6:48 PM 02-13-18

Subject: Bio Update

Barry,

Had to do make a couple of minor edits to the bio. Do you want me to tell Raoul we're good to go?

Jim Conley

Dark Overlord of the Ninth Circle

DEEP Trax Magazine

DARYL FRANKLIN HALL (1586 - 2018), missing since February 27th, 2018 and presumed dead, was last seen skydiving over San Bernadino, New Jersey. Widely regarded as the most technically adept DJ of his generation, Hall's forays into pop music as half of the pop duo 'Hall & Oates' made him a household name across the world. In 1992 Hall commissioned a secret team of scientists to invent the cthonic vibrating fluids now more commonly known as 'radio waves'. Investments in sugar cane left Hall a billionaire at twenty-two and he became as well-known for his philanthropy as his flowing hair. In 1991 he donated the city of Pittsburgh to the city of Dallas and three years later auctioned off his 61 Grammys to pay for a new ozone layer.

A life-long bachelor, he is survived by a cat named 'Maneater' and a thriving ficus.

From: Barry Pfizer

To: Jim Conley

Date: 7:13 PM 02-13-18

Subject: Are you done?

Jim,

I see three options here:

1. I get IT to block your e-mail
2. I charge you with harassment.
3. You stop contacting me forever.

Your call. If I don't hear from you again I'll assume you went with 3.

Good luck and get help

Barry P.

To: Barry Pfizer

From: Jim Conley

Date: 7:40 PM 02-13-18

Subject: What should I do with Daryl?

Barry,

Would you mind if I left Daryl at your place for a few days until I come up with a long-term solution? It would really help out. I don't think I can sleep with a stranger in the house even if he did sing 'You Make My Dreams Come True'.

Jim Conley

Hauptgemeinschaftsleiter

DEEP Trax Magazine

Ps - When should I come down to the office to meet everyone?

To: Jim Conley

From: Barry Pfizer

Date: 8:26 PM 02-13-18

Subject: Daryl Hall is alive and well.

Jim,

Daryl played an acoustic show in Rochester last night. I just watched a clip of it on YouTube. He looks good for 71. Eight thousand people can back me up here - he is not in your dryer. People, even smaller ones like John Oates, cannot fit in a household dryer.

Barry P.

Ps- Most people think I'm a nice guy. Please don't make me do something that's going to change that.

To: Barry Pfizer

From: Jim Conley

Date: 8:35 PM 02-13-18

Subject: The math speaks for itself.

Barry,

The average clothes dryer has a volume of 6 cubic feet. The average human has a volume of only 2.5 cubic feet. With lubricant and pry bars you could easily fit two people in one dryer.

Jim Conley

Graveyard Straw Boss

DEEP Trax Magazine

To: Jim Conley

From: Barry Pfizer

Date: 9:00 PM 02-13-18

Subject: Restraining order

Jim,

I'm trying to be the nice guy here but you just don't want to quit. I've reached my breaking point.

I've asked my attorney to file a restraining order against you tomorrow morning. You've wasted two days of my life and I'm pretty sure you're the most unstable person I've ever come across. This is coming from a man who has interviewed the Unabomber, Aileen Wuornos, Dennis Hopper, David Lynch, Crispin Glover, the guys in Steely Dan, Roman Polanski, Suge Knight. O.J. Simpson, six American presidents, and the entire cast of Jack-Ass.

Please leave me alone before I get the legal system to make you.

Barry P

To: Barry Pfizer

From: Jim Conley

Date: 9:16 PM 02-13-18

Subject: Reaching out

Barry,

A trembling withered arm just tried reaching out for me when I put a fabric softener sheet into my dryer. It was like the last scene of Carrie filmed inside a dryer.

I admit I've been having some fun with you but this time I'm serious. It might not belong to a glitzy celebrity like Hall or Oates but something in there with an arm needs our help.

The air fluff cycle will be done in twenty-five minutes and then I'm going in, with your support or without it.

Jim Conley

Excluded Middle Manager

DEEP Trax Magazine

To: Jim Conley

From: Barry Pfizer

Date: 11:40 PM 02-13-18

Subject: Anything in there?

Jim,

Just getting ready to leave the office (it's been a long long day) and realized you hadn't contacted me in nearly three hours. Thought I'd check in and see how you made out with the arm in your big dryer.

I'm being sarcastic. Most people would get that. With you I can't tell.

Do you make this stuff up as you go along or is it scripted? You might do okay in Hollywood.

Barry P.

To: Barry Pfizer

From: Jim Conley

Date: 11:26 PM 02-13-18

Subject: EXCLUSIVE!

Barry,

The hand was connected to a shoulder connected to a head. The good news is that the head is still moving and in exchange for water and a Mars bar we have an exclusive interview lined up. She's met you and says you did a Weinstein on her at the Grammys back in '94. Probably best if I handle the questions.

She was reported missing on CNN the same day she got here and her ID checks out (that's where I got the birth date from). I know you have concerns about me augmenting the facts so I asked her to tell me her story in her own words instead of relying on any background. This is raw It's a fascinating one and this is going to be one of the best interviews DEEP Trax has ever run.

Sorry things got tense over the last couple days. I get nervous.

Jim Conley

Palatine of Byzantium (ret.)

DEEP Trax Magazine

HELEN "SADE" ADU (1959 -)

The DEEP Trax Interview

DEEP: Thank you for joining us today.

SADE: Can I have water?

DEEP: Soon enough. I thought we'd start where you started - Your childhood. You grew up in an unmapped area of the Pacific, the daughter of an oganesson miner and a glassblower.

SADE: No. I was born in Nigeria. My father was an economics professor. My mother was a nurse.

DEEP: Do you want water or don't you? It's as cold as a glacial tarn.

SADE: What is oganesson?

DEEP: Element 118. Very cutting edge. Unstable like me. Transuranic. Only six atoms of it have been found so far.

SADE: I don't understand. How do you farm something like that?

DEEP: Cautiously. Lets not get caught up by facts. I want to jump back to your childhood. 1926. The slums of Hyderabad. A girl of three finds work as a greyhound jockey.

SADE: I've never been to Hyderabad. What is a greyhound jockey?

DEEP: Sade, we can't run away from our past. I tried and made it less than eighty feet before the sirens started.

SADE: Who are you? You're very strange.

DEEP: Jim Conley, editor-at-large. DEEP Trax Magazine.

SADE: Barry the pig sent you. We're done here. Put me back in the dryer.

DEEP: As soon as my delicates are done. For now, put me in your stirrups, greyhound jockey, and tell me what it feels like riding a dog to victory.

SADE: Why would you want to ride a dog? It's cruel.

DEEP: It's funny.

SADE: A cat riding a dog would be funny. A person on a dog? Not really.

DEEP: What if it was a really short person.

SADE: How short?

DEEP: Your height. Eighteen inches.

SADE: I'm five foot seven.

DEEP: Not anymore. You've been in a dryer for six weeks.

SADE: You're insane. Insane and unusually tall. I want water.

DEEP: Let's talk about your political career. In 2004 You ran for Nigerian Dictator-for-Life and lost to a Vodun fertility idol carved from a hippopotamus spine.

SADE: I said nothing more until you give me water. How tall are you?

DEEP: You're currently single. Experts tell me this is because 99.425% of British men believe you will steal their soul if they look you directly in the eyes.

SADE: Nothing without water. Please don't step on me.

To: Barry Pfizer

From: Jim Conley

Date: 3:07 AM 02-14-18

Subject: Jim Conley

Dear Barry,

This is Sade (I borrowed Jim's laptop). He's upstairs getting water but he'll be back soon so I'll type fast. Your editor is clearly at large. For six weeks he has recklessly used the permanent press cycle while drying delicates such as myself. I am the shrunken aftermath of his disregard and I want his head, even if it does weigh more than I do.

I don't feel safe down here. Jim's cat 'Rich Girl' has been circling and rubbing up against me for nearly a half hour. At five foot seven I wouldn't have even noticed. Now it's like the last ten minutes of 'Alien'. I'm too young to be elegant kibble, Barry. I want this sorted out.

Sade

To: Jim Conley

From: Barry Pfizer

Date: 5:04 AM 02-14-18

Subject: Blue Hats and Bill Shawn

Jim,

The angry soul singer living in your dryer told me to set things straight. I plan to do just that.

Duane Allman and I were snorting coke off Carrie Fisher one Halloween night when he looked over and said 'The man in the blue hat can fly.' I have no idea what he meant by that but it's a great story you can do what you want with.

Here's what I'm going to do.

You've got 48 hours until Friday. Bring me a story and make it a good one. Try to find a few facts to go with it and make sure the words match up with the mouths they came from. Lay it out like a locked-door mystery. It doesn't have to have gun turrets or purebred oranges.

Just slow down long enough to tell people what's really there to see. You write like a night at the carnival but you forget to show what it looks like in the morning.

I thought I was beyond editing. I wasn't. Neither are you.

Barry P.

Ps - Don't even think about calling John Oates. Ever.

To: Barry Pfizer

From: Jim Conley

Date: 4:15 AM 02-14-18

Subject: Deal.

Barry,

Billy Idol has been arrested in Singapore. The word on the street is durian fruit trafficking. Sounds like a DEEP Trax cover to me. I'll call Carol about the flight.

Anybody in the building speak Cantonese or Malay?

I'm going to need to fly business class because of my size (I'm 6'11" and weigh about the same as a Harley Davidson soft tail) so if you have Air Miles this would a good opportunity to cash them in.

Jim Conley

Acting Prophet

DEEP Trax Magazine

Ps - Thank you.

My Demons

Jessica Oeffler

Come forth cruel demons
Display your true form
Come forth
Show me what I've done
Show me where to go
Allow my mind to wander
Give me death
Spare me life
Let me breath
Let me eat
Let me grow
Harden my heart
Don't allow it to beat
Turn it to stone
Push it away
Cast the stone
Into a raging river
Where it will
Eride in time

Come forth cruel demons

Whisper in the night
Come forth
Tell me of omt sin
Tell my body to die
Watch it wither away
Take my life
Give me death
Take the breath from my lungs
My food from the table
Stunt my growth
Make me small
Steal my heart away
Burn it brightly
Into the night
Extinguish the flames quickly
Take the ashes to the plains

Spread them on the wind

Reflections of Insanity

Jessica Oeffler

Reflections of insanity
Stare back into my eyes
Eye to eye I stand today
Face to face with myself
I stand and stare for eternity
Neither lowering their eyes
I stand and stare right back
Looking deeper into myself
I blink first, letting myself win
Never giving myself the credit
Never allowing myself to win
Looking deeper into insanity
Hidden in my very eyes

Sanguine Lactis

By Chloé Agar

Depressing service station music was playing, even though he was not in a service station. He was in a branch of a respectable budget supermarket chain. Every so often, the depressing service station music was interrupted by adverts. He preferred the adverts.

He was pushing his trolley past the fridges of what he fondly called the dairy aisle, but which he had been informed by a staff member some months back was discriminatory against the vegans and lactose-intolerants who used the free-from

products found there. Reaching the milk, he heaped bottles into the trolley. He started with the milk with the blue lids. To this day, he did not understand the significance of the different colours, but he did know that he preferred the taste of the blue.

Once his trolley was full, he went back down the aisle towards the check-out. He drew some looks from the other latecomers in the supermarket as he passed them. He did not blame them. It had been at least a fortnight since he had last washed his hair, for one thing. It was a brown mess that hung greasily down his back to just past his shoulder blades. Those shoulder blades were covered by a knee-length, black leather coat. To finish the look, he was wearing the thickest, widest sunglasses that he had been able to find. Indoors. At night. In truth, he looked like Ozzy Osbourne had found the fountain of youth.

Reaching the check-out, he started to pile milk bottles onto the conveyor belt. The young woman behind the till stared at him, as though it were an affront for him to be using the only till open at this hour while she was dealing with the very important business of twirling her bubble-gum between her teeth and her fingers. Finally, when it became clear that he was committed to buying this trolley full of milk, she started to scan it.

Her eyebrows skyrocketed into her fringe when she saw the total. It was not every day that customers spent over a hundred pounds on milk alone. He produced his card and shoved it into the PIN reader without question, pushing in his PIN with the expression of someone who has done this far too many times before. The whole thing was so unfamiliar to the young woman that she did not even offer the inordinately calorific and sugary chocolate bars sitting beside the till, which were supposed to be a bonus added to any sale. But then, the supervisor who enforced this policy was busy smoking outside, dangerously close to where cars were filling up with petrol. At least, they had been when he had come in.

He left the shop laden with about twenty shopping bags and started to stagger home. Now, he drew even more looks on his walk through Oxford's city centre. Some passers-by who were just drunk enough to be uncoordinated but still extremely helpful stopped to ask him if he wanted help. He waved them away with a polite, tight-lipped smile. Three seconds later, they had forgotten that he existed and were trying to leapfrog bins and bollards. The bags were not too heavy for him. That was a problem that he rarely had. They were just so unwieldy. He resolved, for the hundredth or thousandth time, that he should really start making more than just monthly trips to the supermarket.

The unwieldy bags meant that it took longer than it should have done to cross the centre of Oxford and reach Gloucester Green. This was a wide, red-bricked space that the council had once had the heinous thought to turn into a car park. He was glad that that had never happened. It meant that he still had his cosy flat, surrounded by other cosy flats with well to-do enough residents who did not ask questions. And the Gloucester Green market came three times a week, immediately converting an already quaint space filled with kebab vans, Thai restaurants, and board game cafés into a feast for the senses. Personally, he was fond of the gyoza, but the chap who sold them was starting to get suspicious that this particular customer had not aged in all of the years that he had been serving him.

Shouldering the door open, he wrestled the bags into the kitchen. His kitchen would be an odd affair, to anyone else, considering that he had removed as much as possible and replaced it with extra fridges. Putting the bags down and starting to put the bottles into the fridges, he checked the expiry date on each one and ordered them accordingly. Once he had finished, he shoved the bags into the corner with all of the other bags and went back into his living room with a bottle. Dropping onto the sofa, he fished around for the television remote, found that it had fallen down the back, almost got his hand stuck retrieving it while still holding the bottle in his other hand, and then finally settled. Turning on a customary seasonal re-run of a 1990s comedy series, he sat back and unscrewed the lid.

#

It was while he was lying upside-down on the sofa, with his legs flailing in the air, watching ‘Bridget Jones' Diary’, that he thought that he had reached a new low point. Retrieving the remote from in amongst the empty milk bottles on the floor, he pointed it at the television and changed the channel. He was greeted by the ten o'clock news, which told him two things, neither of which made his evening any better. The first was that he had only been channel-hopping for an hour. The second was that it was the tenth anniversary of the eradication of vampires. Groaning, he turned the television off and rolled to sit upright.

Things really had gone to hell during the Cold War, he felt. Ignoring the irony in that thought, he slumped and stared up at the ceiling and sighed.

“Why,” he asked himself, “couldn't the Soviets have just concentrated on the space race instead of investing in vampires? Then at least hunting us wouldn't have become militarised."

Shuffling, he sat on the remote. The television exploded back into life, scaring the living daylights out of him with an advert telling him that Jools Holland's customary New Year's Eve show on the BBC would start in an hour. Scrabbling and juggling the remote, after a painful couple of minutes he had managed to turn the volume down to something sensible.

He did feel that, if vampires had had to be eradicated, the world could have timed it on a less auspicious day. He had seen enough New Years to know that humans did not need any additional encouragement to enjoy themselves. As the fireworks started, he pulled a cushion over his face and lay there moaning.

Then his phone rang. He could have sworn that it should have been disconnected, seeing as he had not paid the bill for about five years. Swearing, he pushed himself off of the sofa and went over to the phone, narrowly avoiding tripping over the milk bottles in the process. Grabbing the receiver and holding it to his ear, he shouted,

"What? Sorry, what?" He softened his voice and hoped that whoever was cold-calling him was worth the effort.

"You're still alive, then," the voice said, sounding as miserable as he felt.

"In a manner of speaking."

"You know what I mean."

"I think, until you hear otherwise, you can assume I'm alive," he pointed out.

"Mister Caster, you know that we have to check. There are laws dedicated to you, you know."

"And I don't know whether to feel like a pensioner or a terror threat."

"We apologise for the inconvenience, Mister Caster."

He shrugged, even though no one could see him do it.

"You're the ones spending the government's intelligence budget on making annual phone calls to a vegetarian vampire. Tell me, does the prime minister know, or…"

"That will be all for now, Mister Caster." The line went dead.

“So, I have been cut off,” he observed. “Unless MI5 decides to call me, apparently.” Then he paused by the wall and surveyed the room. It was too far beyond a mess to be embarrassing, at this point. Even the debt collectors just stood outside the window and shouted nowadays.

Sighing, he went into the kitchen to get more milk.

#

At twenty to eleven, he weighed up his options. On the one hand, he could stay at home, watching Jools Holland’s show and drinking milk. It was a routine that had served him well for years, after all. On the other, he could go out and join in the festivities. As he was thinking this, there was an especially loud crash from an especially close firework. He sighed. He supposed that it was not just any New Year’s Eve. It was the turn of the millennium, after all. Over the centuries, he had known many people who would have sold their soul to see that.

He did miss them. It was not exactly a realisation, more lifting the lid on denial that he had been steadfastly burying with romcoms of varying quality and the occasional titbit of government service for the last sixty years. The only other immortal he had had to talk to had died then. 1936, he recalled, on a hot July day. That other immortal had been an alchemist, born sometime in the eighteenth century, the exact date of which he neglected to remember. In Spring, or thereabouts. His name had been Hugo Beauwissen, and he had been as pompous as that name sounded, but he had been company. It had never been appealing how he drank the elixir of life like fine wine, as though it was commonplace to have the stuff and Hugo's kind was just more refined than most. But, at the time, the choice had been the alchemist with a stick shoved up an unthinkable orifice, abject loneliness, or the other immortal that he tried not to think about.

She was an imaginara, but a powerful one, powerful enough to keep herself in a youthful body without pills or potions or rituals. He supposed that she must still be alive, although he did everything in his power to avoid being of interest to her. She was the reason that Hugo was dead, after all. He had been hired to kill her at a time when the government had been particularly jumpy about her existence. The last that anyone had seen of Hugo, he had been striding into her house. It was a safe bet that he had not survived very long.

He shuddered. Her name came up occasionally in certain circles, and always so complimentarily. How striking she was.

I suppose that's what comes of having differently coloured eyes. It was certainly one way in which she was memorable. In all of his years on this earth, he had never met anyone else with so starkly differently coloured eyes as she had. One was a brilliant, sky blue and the other was enchantingly grass green. They were hardly subtle.

How sophisticated she was.

I suppose that's what comes of being nobility. Heck, he had heard something a few years ago about how she was a member of the House of Lords.

How wealthy she was.

I suppose that's what comes of this being Oxford. She had been a generous benefactor of multiple colleges for over a century, after all.

Her name had haunted him since he had first laid eyes on the case file for her parents' murder back in the 1870s. In truth, it had stopped being considered a murder when no bodies were found and the blood was reidentified as red paint. The part that bothered him was that she had been the only other person in the house. And he knew better than most what she was capable of with a bit of paint, amongst other things.

He shuddered again.

Lady Rebecca Lillian Greene. She much preferred to go by Beckalily, left over from her childhood. He had spoken face to face with her little, and was glad of it.

And thinking about her brought him back around to thinking about everyone else who had passed on over the last two centuries. It was a terribly vicious circle, he decided, one which really did highlight how un-experimental he had been since being sired. At least there were no more immortals to judge him for his deplorable lack of creativity.

I should be out there, he thought. I should go and see what all of the fuss is about for everyone who can't.

Pushing himself off of the sofa, he shrugged out of his coat and went into the bathroom. Stepping over shampoo bottles that he had meant to recycle at least two years ago, he started to undress. Once his clothes were piled up on top of the toilet cistern, he looked towards the mirror. He still did that, even after so long of having no reflection. Some habits were indeed hard to kick. After a moment, he looked down at himself instead. He was attractive, he knew that much. Vampirism did that to a person. It turned them from an average form of themselves into something better, into the ideal. He had seen people transform from something to whom no one would give a second look into Michelangelo's David. He had certainly been able to get the attention of women when he had felt like it.

Maybe I should try to bring someone back, he wondered as he stepped into the shower. *Or rather, go back with them. I can guarantee that anyone's place has been through less of an apocalypse than mine has.*

Turning on the water, he chuckled. The people that he had used to know – the ones who were long dead and would have done anything the devil wanted just to see the clocks change to midnight tonight – had thought that the millennium would bring the end of the world. They had called it the Rapture. There was a part of him that thought that that would have been preferable to the fireworks detonating outside of his flat. But alas, at least for now he was stuck with the fireworks.

#

Stepping onto Beaumont Street, a wide road with terrible traffic and an excellent theatre that was all of thirty seconds from Gloucester Green, he surveyed the scene. People streaked with glitter and reeking of alcohol wobbled past him. It was one of those rare occasions where the students and the townsfolk were completely indistinguishable from one another. He did not like to hazard a guess as to whether that was a good or a bad thing. A firework exploded somewhere nearby that it should not have been and he started, his ears ringing fit to burst, in a magnificently unsubtle vampiric way by leaping a good ten feet into the air.

Recovering himself and setting off along the street as nonchalantly as he could, given that at least three hundred drunk people had just witnessed his not-so-little indiscretion, he hoped that they were all far too gone to even be able to see any more and that that would be that.

He wandered along the street towards the memorial to the Protestant martyrs burned under Mary Tudor in the sixteenth century. There was a nightclub near to there. It was a small, relatively unappetising underground room, but it would be dark and the sounds of the fireworks would not be able to penetrate the music. Standing beside the memorial, he could hear the music well enough already. It was that mystifying, recent kind of music where he was no longer confident in being able to identify the gender of the artist through a combination of autotune and hormonal uncertainty. Usually, he would not be caught dead there, but women seemed to like that kind of thing. Along with men of a certain persuasion. He did sometimes wonder whether eternity would have been different if he had picked up a male partner along the way, but that sort of thing had never appealed to him and its decriminalisation did not seem to have changed his preferences.

Joining the queue for the club, he tried to ignore the blaring neon lights and pounding music as he was shuffled along in amongst students who already looked to be in varying states of undress. He had long ago decided that it was possible to tell which region of Britain someone was from based on what they deemed to be acceptable nightclub attire in the depths of winter. Trying not to look like a much older man surrounded by women who were barely adults, after a painful amount of shuffling and jostling, he reached the front of the queue.

The bouncer looked like the sort of person even a vampire would not want to upset. He was short, built like one of those roly-poly toys that were popular with children at the moment, and had a face that challenged all comers to do their worst. Holding out a hand calloused from he did not want to think what, the bouncer met his eyes with an expression that was equal parts job-satisfied and furious. He handed over his driving licence without question. It was one of the new-fangled ones with a photograph of the owner. Having no reflection and therefore being impossible to photograph, he had gone to great lengths to have a realistic portrait made and had found that the best person for the job was a street artist in the Montmartre district of Paris. He had figured that having one might come in useful, even though driving had never been his strong suit. The number of cars that he had written off – all in no less than spectacular fashion – in years gone by did not bear thinking about.

The bouncer was looking at him like he was a badger in a chicken-coop. He looked down at the licence again, then back to him. Finally, he said:

"Uriel? That sounds like…"

"It's Biblical," the vampire Uriel Caster snapped as he took back his licence. "Although I appreciate what it sounds like," he added after a moment when the bouncer looked like he wanted to cave this Uriel Caster's teeth into his throat with his impressively polished knuckle-duster.

Moving aside, the bouncer let him pass. Uriel went down the stairs, ducking lower and lower as the ceiling descended to meet him, before emerging onto the dancefloor. It was even smaller and more cramped than he remembered, making him wonder how many people had had the same idea as him and making him feel slightly less ingenious than he would have liked before dealing with humans.

Weaving around gyrating bodies and spluttering with the amount of glitter and hairspray in the confined, airless space, he made it to the bar. Slumping elbow-first onto it, he decided that this was just the sort of experience that would have required him to catch his breath if he still needed to use his lungs.

One of the decidedly harassed bartenders appeared in front of him. Uriel eyed him almost sympathetically before asking:

"You do white Russians here?"

The bartender looked confused, so Uriel made life easier for him:

"Stick some Kahlua in some milk. And bung some cream on top if you have any."

The bartender disappeared to do just that, leaving Uriel in the sense-engulfing haze that was rapidly reminding him why he rarely did this sort of thing any more.

#

An attractive blonde with legs up to her armpits had put her hands in enticing places and lured him onto the dancefloor, still holding his pseudo-white Russian. She was dancing in front of him sensually, being one of those people from a part of Britain where they wear very little clothing to a nightclub. He had to admit that it was an improvement on leaning on the bar drinking a very sorry excuse for a cocktail. Downing what remained of his drink and finding a table occupied by a couple that definitely was not going to notice if he left it there, he joined the blonde with the spectacular legs.

He reciprocated when she put her hands on him again, but gingerly, in case he was right about what she was going to do next.

He was right about what she was going to do next. Coming as close to him as humanly possible, she kissed him. He pulled away quickly, to which she looked anything but impressed. Huffing, she turned and wove away into the throng to find someone more favourable. He felt a pang of disappointment, but reasoned with himself that it was for the best.

"That was unfortunate. But I suppose that it would have been more unfortunate if she had found your fangs."

He spun around to find the most attractive woman that he had ever seen standing behind him, and that was saying something given his centuries of experience of the opposite sex. She was slender, with her legs covered by the tightest black leather trousers that he had never imagined. She was wearing a strapless, glittering pink top that left her midriff exposed. Her skin was whiter than ceramic and her hair – delicately cropped, as was the fashion these days – was blacker than a raven's back. But it was her eyes that were the most exquisite thing about her, the most eye-catching, if he pardoned himself the pun. They were light and bright and clear, even in the dimness and the flashing lights around them. And one was blue and the other green.

Uriel stepped back apace, narrowly avoiding bumping into the back of the blonde with the legs' new beau, with whom she was having significantly more success.

"Lady Greene," he spluttered.

Lady Rebecca Lillian Greene smiled.

"Call me Beckalily," she said before making a sweeping gesture. "Everyone else does."

"Everyone else?"

"I came here with company." As she said this, a young man approached her from behind and wrapped his arms around her. He seemed less articulate than she did and much more intoxicated. "Although," she continued, ignoring him, "I will admit that it is not the most scintillating company."

Taking hold of his hand as it strayed a little too close to a personal place, she met Uriel's eyes. He looked away quickly, but not before the young man had burst into a shower of red glitter, to which drunken students flocked with gay abandon as it dissipated.

"Much better," she remarked as she stepped towards Uriel and tilted his chin up with a delicate fingertip. With her other hand, she smeared his cheek with some of the glitter. "There. Now you look the part."

He spluttered and made to wipe it off, but it would not budge. She laughed. It was a high, tinkling, dainty sound that belied what she had just done most sharply.

"You just killed a man in a public place!" he hissed down her ear.

"There are no witnesses. None who are not dosed up to their eyeballs with alcohol and Lord alone knows what else, anyway. Besides," she added, stepping backwards into what remained of the shower of glitter with her arms spread and letting it cover her, "he is more enjoyable this way."

Uriel did not know whether she was more attractive with the glitter, but he did know that he needed to get away from her if he wanted to keep being the last vampire.

"Uriel," she said gently, catching his expression. She cupped his face in her hands and gazed deeply into his eyes. He tried to look away, but her grip was like marble. Then her eyes flicked to focus on something over his shoulder. “You are not alone.”

“Hm?” he made to turn, but her hands still kept him in place.

“Not very subtle for the last of your kind, are you?” she quipped. “But, by the look of you it has been a while since you were last in public.”

“Hey!”

“Hush, Uriel.” Placing a finger on his lips, she nodded towards the door. “Your friends from intelligence are keeping a weather eye on you, I see.”

He groaned.

“They do that.”

“You will have to tell me how you persuaded the British government to hide you. I never quite caught that part of the conversation.” Laughing again, she released her hold and beckoned him towards the bar.

“You never quite caught…? Beckalily, how closely have you been watching me?”

“Closely enough. You did not think that I would neglect to keep one eye on another immortal, did you? If we can call you that.”

They reached the bar and Uriel raised his hand for the bartender’s attention.

"Oh, don't bother!" she told him, pulling his hand back down. "They are hardly competent, anyway. They would not know the difference between a Merlot and a Moët if they drowned in wine."

Uriel refrained from pointing out that her tastes were probably quite far removed from the average clientele while she snatched up a menu. Laying it on the bar in front of them and opening it, she gestured to the sparkling, heavily doctored images of the cocktails.

"Which one would you like?"

Confused, he shrugged and pointed to one at random.

"Be serious, Uriel. I know that it is not in your nature, but try for me."

He chose a different cocktail with more seriousness.

"You know they're not that good in the flesh, right?"

She eyed him as though he had all of the intellectual fervour of a brain-dead goldfish. Then she laid her palm flat on the image. Raising her hand, a glass brimming with that cocktail came with it. Taking it, she handed it to Uriel, whose jaw was now somewhere between the floor and China. Once he had closed his mouth and taken it from her, she produced one for herself. Sipping it, she nodded appreciatively.

"A fine choice, Uriel."

Reassured that his drink was both real and non-lethal, he sipped it. It tasted sublime, as though all of the doctoring had come with it.

"That is the face of a man who never thought that an imaginara might come in useful," she said with a chuckle.

He continued to sip his drink, staring at her all the while.

#

"Uriel," she said after an amicable silence during which every single bartender had at one point or another come to gawp at their drinks, looked down to see them in their own menu, and had shuffled off again to ask their colleagues if they knew who had made them.

Uriel raised an eyebrow at her and continued to drink while using his glass as an appalling rudimentary shield.

"Shall we leave?" she asked. "The company has improved, but only by one person." She tilted her glass a little towards him.

“I…I suppose.” He stood on tip-toe, squinted into the poorly-placed lights, and peered over the heads of the increasingly lively crowd. Two dark-suited men who looked more out of place than he felt were standing in the doorway, clearly irking the bouncers something chronic. He dropped back down to the flats of his feet.

She pointed towards the toilets.

“We can leave that way.”

“This is MI5 we’re talking about, Beckalily. I don’t think that the bathroom window trick will work.”

Again, the look that suggested that he was a moron.

“How long have we known one another?”

He shrugged.

“Since the 1870s.”

“And have you ever known me to climb out of a window?”

“No, but…”

“Then rest assured that I have no intention of changing that.”

Once they had finished their drinks, she led him over to the ladies’ toilets, pulling him inside at an opportune moment when the lights on the dancefloor had started to flash uncontrollably. She approached one of the mirrors while he hung back, aware of the feet visible beneath many of the cubicle doors. He watched as she placed her palm against the mirror. The glass rippled. Pulling her hand away, she beckoned to him. Taking his hand, she stepped through the mirror. He squawked, earning a response from one of the cubicles. Before the occupant could open the door, he had been dragged through the mirror.

He emerged, his hand still gripped in Beckalily's, in the ladies' toilets of the grand hotel a few doors down from the club. The change in the cleanliness and the calibre of the décor was disconcerting, particularly as she was pulling him out of the toilets before any of the less intoxicated patrons of this venue noticed them.

Leaving the hotel and stepping onto the street, he cast about him. Retrieving his hand from hers, he stared at it, bemused.

"Now, where shall we go?" she asked, brushing her hands against her trousers as though they were a sumptuous gown. Some habits were indeed hard to kick.

As he opened his mouth to reply, eyeing up his options for running along either direction of the street, his throat ran dry. His vision started to blur. Making an odd sort of noise, he fell back against the wall until his head stopped spinning.

"You need to feed," she said, looking at him over her shoulder. "You do not have what could be called respectable staying power, Uriel Caster."

"Hey!" Pushing himself away from the wall, he straightened his coat and ignored the looks that they were receiving from passers-by. "Milk is not as nutritious as blood for us. We need to drink more of it."

"You still say 'we'," she observed. "That is sweet. In that case, I know where we should go."

He nodded.

"So do I."

#

They were sitting opposite one another in one of the unignorably cow-themed ice cream parlours in the city. They usually closed at eleven o'clock, but had made an exception for the New Year that was bringing in the new millennium.

Each had in front of them a paper cup brimming with ice cream of spectacular and outlandish flavours. Uriel was devouring his like it was the elixir of life itself, while Beckalily was taking a much daintier approach.

After a while, once Uriel was feeling much more like himself again, he looked up. She was staring back at him, licking the ice cream on the end of her wooden spoon with the very tip of her tongue. He looked down again.

"What is it?" she asked, sliding the rest of the ice cream into her mouth with her lips and burying the spoon back in the scoop. "You want to ask me something. I can tell."

"How do you do it?" he asked, trying and failing not to look at her. She tilted her head to one side and continued to stare at him. "How to you keep young? You're no vampire or alchemist. And imaginari never live longer than any other human normally. I read up on it after Hugo…" he trailed off meaningfully and managed to meet her eyes.

"Normally," she repeated. She leaned forward, her voice developing a conspiratorial tone. "You and I both know that that does not apply to me." She leaned back, a smile forming on her lips. "I can pass through mirrors. Most imaginari struggle to do that. But I can do it with ease." She chuckled. "The eyes are mirrors, if you think about it."

Uriel started to look uncomfortable.

“I take people’s bodies,” she said bluntly. “I pass into theirs, remove the occupant, and voila. With a little tweaking here and there to look like myself again, of course. My house is full of portraits of myself,” here she indicated herself with a grand gesture, “and photographs, now that they are polychrome. It is like painting a canvas, but more magnificent.”

“And what do you do with the…occupants whom you remove?”

“They are part of my collection,” she waved her hand dismissively. “Most things become stone when petrified, but souls…Souls are infinitely more beautiful. They become glass. I have moved them into their own special place recently. It was a great improvement. I am disappointed that it took me so long to do it.”

“Is that what happened to Hugo? When he went into your house?”

“In fairness, he did come to kill me,” she reminded him, her voice hardening. “You were fortunate that you refused to accompany him, otherwise I would have been spoiled for choice.” Her voice softened again: “But yes, that is what happened to him.”

“And is that…” he could barely choke the words out, “Is that Hugo’s body?”

She looked down at herself, ran her hands from her hips to her chest for a moment, and then looked back to him with an impish grin.

“No. It lasted better than most, given how much of the elixir of life that he drank, even for an alchemist, but it has been over sixty years. I have moved on since then. This one,” she looked down again, “was a model. Italian, I believe.” Looking up and seeing his quizzical expression, she elaborated: “I was attending Paris Fashion Week. I know, not something that I would normally do. It is a long story involving some exquisite paintings that the Louvre was foolish enough to leave unguarded. The model did show an interest in me,” she added ruefully, “but women have never been my cup of tea.”

“You’ve never experimented?” he asked, taking another scoop of ice cream. It was strawberry with a suitably euphemistic name. “You’ve lived long enough.”

She eyed him almost pityingly as she too took another scoop of ice cream. Hers was brilliant blue. Oxford blue, the parlour called it. It was blueberry.

“Lord, no,” she said, swallowing. “I know what I like, thank you. Not that I ever had the disincentive of it being illegal. Just dreadfully frowned upon.” She laughed in a way that told him exactly what she thought of that nonsense and which encouraged a family sitting nearby to shuffle away from them.

He nodded thoughtfully.

“Then why were you out with those people? Those students?”

She rolled her eyes and flicked ice cream at him. It missed and landed on the table an equal distance between them.

“I was bored. I have studied as many degrees as I wish at this university. Now I want company.”

“You have plenty of friends at home,” he reminded her. “They’re not so imaginary for you as they are for everyone else.”

“Yes, and I love them dearly, but they are not human. I have not been out since the sixties. And that was a mistake,” she added with a grimace. “And,” she added after a moment of contemplatively twirling her spoon in her ice cream, “I wanted to see the new millennium. People did used to talk about it so. The ones whom we knew.”

"I know who you mean. And they did."

"And you?" She looked pointedly at him.

"The same," he admitted. "I don't think I've been out except to the supermarket for at least five years, better ten."

"Since vampires were eradicated," she said.

He cast about them, but the family was getting up to leave anyway. Otherwise, they were alone save for a small group of very drunk people in the corner.

"Yes, since then."

"I did wonder why they did not kill you. Presumably because you have not touched blood for – what is it? – two hundred years?"

"Close enough."

"And the fact that you have helped the British government in more ways than it would like to admit. I did enjoy that."

"That as well."

"Precisely what did they have you doing?"

He looked uncomfortable but told her:

"Some work during the Second World War. Mainly about the Enigma machines. And I did some useful things during the Cold War, as well."

"How ironic."

“I know,” he agreed with a grimace. “But they granted me immunity for it. Which means that they follow me around and waste a lot of money and time.”

“But presumably they will kill you if you drink blood?”

He nodded.

“They added an entire sub-section to some obscure laws about the supernatural specifically for me. I am honoured, but I think I’m more embarrassed.”

She laughed.

A bang outside alerted them to the increasing intensity of the fireworks. The parlour was not far from University Parks, a large, open, green space full of trees and with a duckpond and a river. It was a fine place to set off fireworks.

“Do you want to go and watch them?” Beckalily asked, checking the clock on the parlour’s wall. “It is ten to midnight.”

“Alright.” Pushing his chair away, Uriel stood. He went around the table to help pull Beckalily’s chair back for her, but she was already standing by the time that he got there.

“I appreciate the gesture,” she told him as they left, “but it is hardly necessary.”

#

The fireworks were spectacular, and there was still no sign of the Rapture. Uriel chuckled to himself as the bells of the nearby churches tolled midnight. He could think of many people whom that would have annoyed. They had been an odd bunch, he recalled. People had become much less interesting since the Victorian period, he felt.

As the fireworks cracked and burst above them, he became aware of Beckalily's arm threading through his. Her head met his shoulder as she gazed upwards.

Once the fireworks were subsiding, he looked down at her.

"I'm still afraid of you, you know."

"You are wise to be," she replied, turning her gaze to him. "Remember what I did earlier." She reached up to touch the glitter that was still on his cheek.

"I don't need reminding," he promised, taking hold of her wrist and lowering her hand away from his face as the crowd started to disperse.

Once they were as good as alone, Beckalily said:

"That was all rather underwhelming."

"It was," he agreed. Looking over to where some other people remained, he shrugged. "Maybe it had more resonance for people who weren't hoping for the world to end."

"Maybe." She sighed and cast about them, her eyes needing more time to adjust to the dark than his did. "I would have quite liked the world to end. It would have been a change."

"It would."

They started to walk away, back to the streets and the colleges.

"Will you go home now?" he asked.

"I imagine so."

"And not come out for another thirty years?"

She laughed.

"We shall see."

#

Parked by the kerb on the road that Uriel and Beckalily were following back into the city centre was a suspicious black car. The occupants of the car were staring through the windscreen, shaking their heads and wondering exactly how they should phrase the call that they were about to make to their superior.

Eventually, one of them picked up the phone and started the call.

"Yes?" The voice at the other end sounded exhausted – from the festivities or work, the occupants of the car did not want to guess.

"We may have a problem, sir," the occupant holding the phone started delicately.

"What kind of problem?"

"A Uriel Caster kind of problem, sir."

"Oh?" The voice was now strained and apprehensive.

"He and Lady Greene are being…close."

The voice at the other end swore colourfully.

"Where are they?"

"Heading into the centre. Towards his flat, by the look of it."

"Then tail them. And, if he takes her inside that flat, you know what to do."

There was silence.

"Gentlemen? Gentlemen?"

There was a scream and the line went dead.

Back in Oxford, there was now an extremely realistic graffito of a black car with two black-suited occupants on the road. Standing over it, Beckalily smiled before striding back along the pavement to where Uriel was waiting, tactfully trying not to look. She slipped her hand into his and they carried on walking.

END

She said stop it

You’re seeing spots

I replied to the Sun

They’re tearing into hearts

We missed outta turn

Onto another page

Finalizing our rage

What we see in the privy ain’t

The “Know”

(She’s a little tricky)

By: Donnie Disruptor

Stygian Heart

The child was born after midnight. Lord Jennalise, the handsome, rakish father, had found no good answer to his questions, despite a massive expenditure of time and coin. He stalked the halls of the great house, fuming at the few savants still in his employ, pupils wide with a worry he would not share. Lady Jennelise had suffered tremendously. Horrific nightmares plagued her sleep. Morning sickness began early, the pain in her stomach lasting throughout. By the time the delivery came, she was a hollow wretch of a woman, worn by fatigue, cramps and nausea. Maids whispered that the child was cursed, but such talk was the source of many dismissals and those who thought it (even the house guard) came to know better than to speak openly.

Guards stood their positions, fidgeting in their armor, their strength doubled for the delivery, as if the young lord was expecting an attack. Maids hid in their rooms or hurried back and forth, delivering clean towels and hot water. They did their best for their lady, answering the demands of the most talented midwife available.

It was not enough. Lady Jennallise screamed in agony as the child crowned, and died. The midwife cried out as the child fell from the birthing canal, dropping it into the fresh, hot towels gathered at the mother's waist. The babe was perfect, brilliant blue eyes opening and looking from a heart-shaped face around the room with a startling prescience. From the knees down, however…

Hearing the death cry, Lord Jennallise let out a howl and a curse, calling a name that stuttered off his lips and caused the nearest guards to wince with sudden headaches. One young maid fell to the floor, going into a paroxysm of spasms that broke both of her arms, cracked several teeth and left her deaf and dumb for the rest of her days. Eyes aflame, he burst into the delivery room with a handful of picked guards and proceeded (it was said later) to slaughter the midwife and every servant involved.

To the world, the child was stillborn, the mother lost in birth.

Lord Jennallise fell into a dark humor from which he never recovered. Servants were dismissed, along with several of the guards, many of whom claimed a darkness had settled over the house. The mercantile prowess of House Jennallise fell into a decline from which it never recovered. The young, handsome lord ceased to manage his affairs with any real effort. Contracts were ignored or forgotten. Deadlines were missed.

Years after, the name of House Jennallise was whispered as one cursed.

Sunlight dappled the forest floor in crazed patterns of greens, browns and brilliant bits of dust suspended in the air. Tenerife held, silent as the tree against which she leaned, bowstring pulled to her cheek, bow held out, barbed arrow against her pointing finger. The buck had wandered into her range some minutes ago, but still her master had refused to let her arrow fly, waiting instead until it was within killing range.

“To fire early is to injure needlessly,” he had taught her. “The creature you maim could run away faster than you can, live on beyond your reach only to die of infection and blood poison from your impatience. Peace, calm and tranquility will bring about the killing shot. One arrow. One kill. No pain.”

Still, impatience and the strain of muscle fatigue wore at her and she wished only to let fly. But he was watching from not far away, invisible against the forest in a cloak of doeskin and leaves. She would not fail this test, for it was her last.

“I am your master in your studies,” he had told her. “I will teach you what I know, in the hope that you can learn to master not just these skills but yourself.”

“I know no one else,” she had replied. He was father, guide, guardian, teacher. There was no one else in this portion of old growth woods for leagues. “I have seen no one else.”

“That is for your own safety.”

“Why?”

“Trust me,” he had answered with his sad smile, stroking the slender curving horns protruding from her forehead. “It is for the best.”

It was when he was feeling lowest that he stroked her, she had long since learned. It was a loving, gentle caress, but one that only served to highlight the differences between them. She had horns. He did not. She had a short, slender tail that whipped about when she was angry or emotional. He did not. Her legs were animal-like, sweeping back at the knee to another joint that aligned her lithe calf with a small black hoof. He had no second joint and his feet were obnoxious long things that wiggled at the end and stank when he wore his boots too long.

The buck crossed the invisible line she knew was the killing range and she saw him nod. The arrow loosed, singing across the clearing to bury itself in its heart, killing it in an instant. Her exhausted arms slumped and she leaned heavily against the tree before rushing in to finish the work.

She heard his words, though he spoke not, his teachings echoing in her mind. “In case the arrow does not kill, you must slit the throat and end its pain so that it will not suffer. All the while, you must whisper the litany I taught you.”

“In your honor,” she whispered, rushing soundlessly across the clearing, knife coming loose from its scabbard. “In your death, there is life. In your cold, there will be warmth. In your passing, there will be peace.” She drew the blade across the animal’s throat, slitting it though she could tell from the glazed look that the beast had died immediately. Only then did she move to examine the kill.

He was a handsome one. A fourteen point antler rack atop his head, a beautiful coat of tan fur ranging to white around his belly, with black lines just beneath his eyes. His eyes, while he had been alive, were a deep golden color that made her think of sunsets. She began to clean the kill as her master slid from his hiding place and moved to crouch nearby, wordlessly watching her efficient movements. Only when the animal had been properly butchered, skinned and its meat packaged for travel did he stand and move to her side.

"Well struck and done," he said quietly. He took her into his embrace and held her for a long moment. "I have taught you all that I know." His sad eyes held the faintest smile as he put his arm around her and began to walk.

"Thank you, master," she whispered, momentarily overcome with emotion. Was this goodbye?

"Tonight, we will feast on your kill and I will answer those questions you have asked for so long, as I have promised.

Her eyes widened as she realized that he was sad not only because she had learned everything he had to teach her, but because whatever it was he had promised to tell her would, like as not, mean the end of their time together. He was not her father, after all. She had asked the question thousands of times, but he would not answer. Tonight would change everything she knew.

They fell into a companionable silence as they went, his mind on the ramifications of what he was to tell her, hers on the potential outcomes that might come from hearing it. They jerked out of it a short time later when the sounds of the forest went silent and they found themselves staring face to face with a pack of wolves drawn by the scent of blood.

“Seven,” he whispered. “Too many to scare off. Too many to fight. Too hungry to care about the threat two humanoids might offer defending their catch.”

Before she could react, one of them lunged at her with a snarl, the others moving to encircle them both. She dodged to one side, dropping the meat packets in their still bloody wrappings and reaching for the knife she used to skin the kill. Her master had gone for his bow, burying an arrow in the side of one wolf and dropping it before two others lunged his way. Too soon, however, she was forced to ignore him in favor of her own imminent danger.

The first wolf lunged again, catching her weapon arm in its jaws and clamping down. A scream of pain escaped her, staggering at the heavy weight of the animal as it attempted to pull her down and make an easy kill of her. Two other wolves shot in from the sides, hoping to take advantage of her situation, drag her down and rip her throat out.

“No!” she cried, the knife falling from suddenly paralyzed fingers. She heard it hit the soft loam, every sound amazingly loud and clear. The panting of the hungry wolves, the snap of twigs as her master fought for his life nearby. The grinding of her forearm bones as the wolf struggled to bring her down. She felt the pain throughout her body, lightning fast.

Blood poured from the tear in her skin, bright red, hot. Another beast hit her from behind, sending her staggering forward, the weight of the first wolf pulling her down. Her legs struggled to compensate for the added weight and failed. She buckled, fell to the ground. She felt a wolf dig into the leathers of her left thigh, heard the snarl and yip of the others as they felt the kill coming. Felt blood on her cheek as another leapt on her prone form and tore into the skin at her neck, trying to strangle her, to break her neck.

Blackness bore in. Pain, rage, fear, all building into an overwhelming, flickering sense of…

Not right.

Pain stroked throughout her body, a blinding shriek of agony that shuddered throughout her limbs, coruscated through her torso, lit her from within with a flaming eruption that threatened to rip her into pieces. Her mind shut down, seeing the world as if through a long tunnel, the light far away. Her fingers hurt. They felt twice as long and… edged…

Not right.

Darkness settled in and the distant light faded away entirely.

The fire was banked for the evening, the skin cleaned and hung out to dry in the fresh night air. The meat had become an incredible stew that, along with wild rice and a number of vegetables they had grown in their small garden throughout the summer, had entirely filled them up and left them comfortable and warm. They sipped the golden amber liquid he kept for significant moments as he sat across the fire, eyes staring through her at some distant memory. She toyed with her own glass, watched the liquid swirl about as she spun it this way and that. She lost track of time, liquor fumes working their way through her tired mind…

She jerked back into focus at the sound of his shout, eyes widening as she realized the glass was floating in the air in front of her, her hands in her lap. It fell as soon as she made eye contact with it, spilling its amber contents and crashing to the dirt.

She looked up from trying to catch it to find him staring at her. There was more white to his eyes than color. It took a moment to realize it for what it was. fear.

"Master?" she asked, looking from him to the glass and back.

"Don't do that," he said, shaken.

"Do what?" *A flash. Pain shattering throughout her body. Wolves flung bodily into the air…*

She shuddered, blinking the image away.

"You've done that several times in the last few days," he said quietly, worriedly.

"Done what?" *Blood flying. Anger overwhelming. Shattering bones between her fingers. Black claws instead of fingers. Shredding fur and flesh as if nothing…*

He shook his head, blinking slowly. He put his hands in his lap, held them there as if to keep them from shaking. His eyes were returning to normal as he gazed at her. "It must be true, then," he whispered.

“What must?” she asked. Her head and shoulder ached, as if she had fallen on it…

No… As if…

Torn. Shredded. Bloody…

She blinked. What was happening? She reached up to touch her unharmed shoulder and head, a phantom ache persisting there.

“Everything,” he answered. He picked up his glass and threw the last drop back before pouring himself another. That one followed the first before he sat back and resumed watching her.

“You are scaring me, master,” she said worriedly. He, and whatever was happening to her…

“I am scaring YOU,” he said, chuckling.

“Have I done something wrong?”

“No. No. You have done what you were meant to do, I think.” He did not think she caught the added whisper, “Regardless of all that I have done…”

“Master? Is something wrong?” she asked again. “What was I meant to do?”

He laughed, the skin of his cheeks taking on a reddish glow that she had never seen before. His eyes were dilating again and he seemed… strange… She noticed that his hands were bandaged. She did not remember him getting hurt.

Wolves. Terror. Blackness. Pain. So much pain…

She winced at the memory of something she could not clearly recall. "Master?"

"You have… come of age, Tenerife. Your time of ascendancy is upon. Time is having its way, regardless of… well… regardless."

"I do not understand."

"You would not. How should I say this, child? You are not the same as I…"

It was her turn to laugh. "I know as much, master," she said, grinning. She reached up to stroke one of her horns pointedly.

"Well, there is a reason for that. A reason I have kept hidden from you all these years. One that it has come time to share."

She quirked a brow, intrigued at his sudden openness. Was it the amber liquid, or was there something more to this? Had she earned this by shooting the buck? Was it the floating glass? What had brought this on?

"I have never told you how we came to be together, Tenerife. It has been a question you have asked from time to time, but one I have never been willing to answer."

She nodded, remembering. All those times, he had waved her off. "Another time," he'd said. "Perhaps."

"It is not possible for one to remember the circumstances of their own birth, but yours was… rather special, to say the least." He laughed mirthlessly. "Not that everyone around was not aware of it by the time… well…" He faded off, poured another drink, shot it back.

"You are scaring me, master. Is this something I will not want to know later?"

Pain… Blackness rushing in. A tunnel of darkness with light at the end. A brilliant flame erupting… Wolves again… This time, flying away from her in sprays of blood, torn open, flayed with a stroke of her claws…

Claws?

He smiled, this time truthfully, and eyed her. "I have always appreciated that about you, child. Always straight to the point. I like that. Most do not ever reach that sensibility. One reason I live out here, alone with you. At least, until now…" He faded off, staring at his glass.

"Master?"

He jerked, as if pulled back from whatever precipice he had been considering. “Your birth. I was talking about your birth… Yes… Well… Not all who are born do so under such circumstances as your own, child. You are, as we have always known, not the same as I. Not the same as… Well… any, so far as I know.”

“Any?” She cocked her head, considering.

“Child, you are unique. Most who walk this world are like I, if only in general. There are only a few that would claim to come close to you, and they are of the… fey… persuasion.”

“The forest nymphs? We offer our valedictions to them. I am like they are?”

He smiled. “Yes. Those. The satyrs, more particularly, but you are not of fey origin… At least, it is not often considered that, though there is no proof.”

A great fury… A great darkness… Dark filled with flames… A shadowy shape with glowing eyes… Eyes that seemed to stare at her… through her… see everything and know everything… Who she was… What she was… Who she would be…

“Wolves are as nothing to you, child.”

“Wolves?” she asked, woozy.

"Wolves?" he said sharply, adjusting his position. "I said nothing about wolves…" His eyes took on an anxious look. His glance to one side drew her attention. There was a pile of bloody bandages lying there, the shreds of his hunting garb gathered in a pile.

"Lies… All of it… You are something else, child. Something meant for greatness… Your greatness…"

"Greatness?" she asked, confused. Why did her master have two voices?

His eyes grew wider. "Child! Focus on me! Ignore what you are hearing and focus on me!"

"What?"

"He lies… He wishes to keep you weak… Kill… Kill him…"

Her master was kneeling before her, hands on her face, holding her close to his own. "Look at me, Tenerife! LOOK at me!"

Darkness filled with fire… Those eyes, glittering in the dark with malicious glee…

Dark eyes looked into hers, wide with fear, but determined nonetheless. Worry mixed with care. Was it… love… she saw?

"Master?"

“You are so hot,” he whispered. Still, he pulled her close, wrapped her into a hug. “It was wrong of me to keep this from you. It has come time…” He stood, pulling her with him. “Come with me.”

“Lies… Kill…”

She followed, as she always had, but there was something in her that demanded he stop wasting time and just *tell* her!

“Tell me,” she said harshly.

“I am telling you, Tenerife, but you must come with me. Ignore what you are hearing except for my voice. See only my face, child. Follow me.”

She nodded, head aching. A burning fire had started in her stomach and was spreading throughout her body. A hideous aching pain that threatened to overcome her senses. She felt that tunnel opening again, saw the world disappearing…

“Tenerife!”

She jerked, opening her eyes again. Master was taking her to the pool where they bathed after their hunts. She remembered she had been there earlier that day…

After the hunt…

The buck… The blood…

The wolves…

"Oh," she whispered, eyes widening. The blood...

"Yes... Kill..."

Master could be killed with a simple blow to the back of his neck. It would knock him senseless and she could twist his neck like she did the grouse they ate for dinner during the winter months. It would be so easy. She could feel his flesh between her fingers, hear the bones crunching as they snapped...

The cold was a shock to her heated skin. It surrounded her, covered her, filled her mouth, nose and ears. The cold sensation utterly shut off the heat burning within. She rose from the water of the grotto and stood, startled and embarrassed.

Master was standing on the old stone that overhung the pool where they bathed, massaging his neck.

"Tenerife! Tenerife!" he called worriedly. "Child!?"

"Yes, master?" she asked, confused. "Where... How did I..." She was still dressed, but not in her hunting garb. She remembered that now. They fight with the wolves. The black claws that had come from her fingers, shredding them after they'd begun to kill her slowly, ripping chunks out of her thighs and shoulders. She had felt the flames rile up from within, burn through her body, fill her mind with fury. She had cast them off, thrown them as they were mere pups instead of fully grown killers. She had shattered three of them in as many heartbeats, pulled two off her master and tossed them into the trees, hearing their yelps of pain with a sense of murderous glee…

“What is happening!?” she cried, terrified. “Master!?”

“You are the daughter of Lady Cairalleiu Jennellise, child,” he called to her. “Said by many to have been cursed with the taint of the abyss in your blood. Child of Lord Heironymous Jennellise, great grandchild of the union between demon and your great great grandsire! You are feeling the blood awakening, despite all that I have done…”

“All you have done?” she asked, eyes wide as she looked around with a newfound terror of everything. “What are you saying?!”

“I found you that night in the woods,” he said, words pouring out in a torrent from lips that had held them back for years. “You were a crying babe, alone in the forest atop the sacrificial stone! You were perfect! Beautiful! Your legs made me think of the satyrs. I thought you might have been left by them as an offering to the forest gods… I… I took you in…”

“A demon?” she said, mind processing too slowly.

“A demon, child. You are the great grandchild of a demonic union. Your father hid it away, forgot the truth. He searched all the while of your mother’s pregnancy, but could find nothing to stop what he knew to be the truth!”

“The truth?”

“That you are born tiefling! A child of the Abyss!”

“Child of the…”

“All is not lost, child! I have done what I can to teach you! Reminded you of what there is to be had. That life is a precious thing! Not to be thrown away in pointless violence!”

“I… I know,” she whispered.

“You are there, inside,” he said, touching his breast. “You are not a demon’s plaything, child. You are your own being, with your own thoughts, mind and heart! You are YOU! You are my apprentice! The daughter I wish I had! My daughter! Mine!”

He howled the last words into the dark forest night, pain filling his every fiber.

“Daughter?” she asked, eyes wide in the darkness of the pool. “Your daughter?”

He leapt down with a splash and moved to take her into a hug. “Yes. My daughter. You are a child of the forest, Tenerife. Never forget what I have taught you. Never forget what you have learned about life and how it is intertwined…"

"Kill…"

"Kill?" she asked softly.

"What?" her master cried. "What!?" He pulled her tighter against his breast, crushing her into him as if his mere presence could shutter the storm at war within her mind.

"He is dark…" she whispered. "But his eyes are so bright…"

"Ignore him, Tenerife! He is not real! He is not your future! He does not have to be anything!"

"Lies…"

She screamed. The cold water warred with the heat within. The fire shuddering through her was too much.

Darkness surrounded her. Warmth covered her.

Arms. They are arms.

"No… Blood…"

Hellfire roared from black craters in the everlasting night, coals flashing down from a frighteningly dark and hellish sky. Lava lapped at her waist. The demon held her close…

Water… Master…

Screams echoed through the forest night, a woman's at first, followed by a deeper man's voice, raised in terror and then…

Pain…

The sunlight dappled the forest floor in crazed patterns of greens, browns and glittering bits of dust suspended in the air. The old path led to the edge of the forest, where the populated lands lay. Master had gone there before to trade skins and meat for the supplies they needed in the deep forest. She had never been allowed to go with him before, but that was about to change. There was no master in her life. Neither dark nor light. She was her own person now. She would go where she would go, and she would make her own way.

The sunlight beyond the trees was bright. A thin line of smoke marked the first settlement over the hills, not far away. She stepped out, shading her eyes, and blinked…

Tera Mamoru - Catechism

The world was fire. Everywhere she looked, flames filled the distance. Small, intensely dark areas were interspersed between the brilliant orange/yellow, leading her to believe that there might be no floor at all. Crackling flames and rippling laughter competed for her attention, drawing her gaze this way and that. Were those eyes in the flames or was that her imagination? Hot… It was so hot…

Tera woke, sitting bolt upright and wide-eyed. Sweat dappled her ice-white skin, gathering in the folds and ripples of her ridged forearms and shins. It dripped down her face, burning her eyes when it caught in her lashes. The room was freezing around her.

This was the third such nightmare in as many days. They'd started just a day after her arrival at the temple. The three priests responsible for keeping it up only letting her in after she declared her purpose as a traveling *onmyoji* for the Imperial Inquisition and showed them the gold and silver tattoo that took up the majority of her back. Demons and devils could not bear the touch of the silver holy symbol she wore on her breast, but that was not always proof for the suspicious. Metals could be faked.

Such could not be said about the tattoo. The blade tip ended at the top of her buttocks, the pinions of the Western-style cross guard reaching just beneath her shoulder blades. The pommel sat just below her hairline. The entire thing was done in gold and silver ink and glowed in the light. No demon could bear such a thing in their skin. Most of the time, it lay hidden beneath her long white hair and the knee-length cloak that covered her back. The priests, as in many cases before, saw the tattoo when she turned to expose it and were relieved to find that the red-horned, sapphire-eyed woman at their doorstep was indeed one of the good guys.

And then there was her name: Tera Mamoru. "Protector of the Temple." Not exactly the name of a demon. Even the thickest-skulled had to recognize that disparity, if the holy symbol and tattoo did not force them otherwise.

She had reason to be grateful. It was winter in Minkai. The snows had fallen early and coated everything in a thick, muffling blanket of white. She'd found a mountainside temple, announced her presence and asked for succor. It was with trepidation that they let the demonic woman into their hallowed halls – and the warmth that came with them. A small coal-and-incense burner sat in one corner, trying hopelessly to heat the chamber. Ice had formed a rime on the tabard she wore as her only clothing, hung as it was on a rack nearby. The red ropes she used to tie it to her body were coiled at its base. They too were caked in a thin layer of ice. Alone among the items in the room, her cold-iron-forged demon-slaying blade she carried with her had no accumulation of icing covering it. It stood upright on a metal stand, glowing of its own accord.

Wistfully, she thought back a month prior, to just before the first true chill of winter. She had helped a village elder free his daughter's soul from the torment of a demon. The air had been cool then, but not uncomfortable. The cool breezes of fall seemed utterly furnace-like to the cold winds of winter.

But she was so hot! She tossed her blanket aside to let the air cool her, but only for a moment. The cold was painful. She stared at the ceiling in dismay. Laying a forearm across her head, she tried to think.

The Venerables in the main chamber of the temple had seemed to glow in the golden light of oil lanterns as she was led there to abase herself before them. The great statue had stared above her, one hand at its waist holding a lotus, the other raised in a sign of benediction. Upon its presentation by the monks, she had said her prayers, noticed the ferocious glare of the sword-wielding Venerable staring her down, and suppressed a shiver before leaving to accept a bowl of warm gruel and a plate of fried fish on rice. A hot tea had washed it down and she thanked the priests for their generosity.

"Until such time as the roads become passable, I will be staying here," she told them. "I will stay out of your way and meditate until such time." The holy symbol guaranteed their obedience to her request, but she was grateful nonetheless. While she did not feel the cold as much as the rest of the people of Minkai, even she was growing weary of trudging through the growing snow drifts to get from place to place.

They led her to a room, offered a pallet to sleep on and a blanket. One of them had set the coal-and-incense burner to warm her personal space, and left her.

A pair of brass statues of the Venerables stood at the base of a small recessed area. A long scroll hung in the recess, depicting a long mountain slope and a white bird with black tipped feathers. A trio of red berries decorated the bottom left of the scroll, just above the square stamp identifying the artist. Beneath it sat a small bowl filled with amaryllis flowers, evincing a warmth that did not extend to the rest of the tatami-floored space.

The fever dream faded until it was replaced with the dull ache of mid-winter's chill. Unable to sleep, she became restless.

The mountain temple was famous for the hot springs located just below. After staring at the ceiling for a while, she decided she would try to warm herself in them. It was the middle of the night. No one would be there. None could complain about her appearance if no one was awake to notice.

Rising, she cracked the rime of ice from her tabard and drew it on before bending to pull the red rope into position about her waist, lashing the falls of cloth to her body. It left her limbs and back bare, highlighting the purple tinge of her limbs. Her snow-white skin was left visible, making her presence impossible to ignore. Villagers were often terrified by her unnatural appearance; the ridged forearms and shins, the long red horns protruding from either side of her head.

She made no effort to hide them. She was, after all, a walking lesson. She was a human-demon hybrid. Marked with the seal of Inquisition and sent into the world to find and destroy the demons who threatened the people of Minkai.

"After all, who better to dispel a demon than one with demonic blood in their veins?" She had repeated her old master's favorite rhetorical question many times since leaving his side. It seemed to calm even the most terrified peasant (assuming she could get a word in edgewise).

Dressed, she slid the door aside and stepped into the (if possible, even colder) hallway. The wood floor was polished from years of careful attention by the priests who lived here into a brilliant sheen, catching even the barest light of the candle at the end of the hall and reflecting it in a long reddish-gold glow. Creeping slowly, so as not to awaken or startle the sleeping monk in the next room, she moved down the hall and around the corner leading to the front of the temple.

The old man snored gently as she passed and she could not hide the smile that flickered across her features. At least he was sleeping now. The first day he had not slept at all, afraid she might leap up and devour him in the night.

The heavy wooden doors of the side entrance were knotted closed against the weather. Untying them, she slid one open and felt the first frozen wind of the night. It sent a chill through her, but faded quickly. She was usually unfazed by the weather, but this winter had been harsh and even she was feeling the cold. Knowing she should be frozen stiff at its touch, her thoughts went back to the dream…

Fire flickered in the back of her eyes when she closed them. Perhaps that was the reason? Was it a warning? A premonition, perhaps? She had experienced such things in the past. It would not be the first time.

Stepping onto the snowy stones outside, she slid the door back into position, whispering a soft prayer of contrition for having left it untied against the night. The path to the hot springs was lined with small statues representing priests who had served at the temple over the years and had passed on. Covered with snow except for the small red bibs tied as ritual clothing to protect them against the weather, they receded down the mountainside, off to one side of the main approach. The stepping stones were icy, but she clenched her toes and the black claws that extended from them gave her excellent purchase. Another would have slipped and fell.

“Thank you oh kami, for the small blessings that I have been given,” she uttered, feeling the talons break through to secure her steps.

Clouds of vapor announced her approach to the hot springs. The naturally heated water resisted freezing even in the dead of winter, creating vast clouds of vapor that never faded in the winter chill. A high bamboo wall encircled the bathing area and she pulled the section tied across the entrance aside before slipping silently through.

She might not feel the cold, but her body reacted as a normal person’s would. Her skin, exposed to the cold elements had tightened, noticeable in the pinch around her eyes, the cold tightness about her nose, the dry, scratchy feel of her body beneath her tabard. She felt it soften as the moist heated air enveloped her and sighed in pleasure.

A bronze statue of one of the Venerables guarded either side of the arch leading to the baths beyond, expressions fierce but only against those not allowed to enter. Within, wicker baskets held towels and piles of sponges. Using a finger talon to crack the ice, she pulled forth a cloth and a sponge and shed her uniform, placing it in a lidded basket which she set on the floor.

Naked, she stepped into the mist-filled space beyond the archway.

When the priests were awake, they kept the baths lit with thick tallow candles that took hours to burn down. Those candles had been put out and the foggy baths were dark. As in the temple, however, Tera could see without issue, her heritage having granted her the ability to see clearly in even the darkest conditions. Slipping into a pool, she dipped her frozen wash cloth into the water and smiled as it softened. The sponge followed and she made her way to a set of stones piled high in one corner of the spring where she could sit and enjoy the heat soaking throughout her body.

Leaning her head back against the stone, she laid the cloth over her chest and slid down until her nose was just above the surface. Steam filled the area in billows of white that would make it impossible to see were she not gifted with the ability to see regardless. No one knew she was here. No one was about.

No one would be terrified of the demonic manifestation she appeared to be.

She was safe.

She closed her eyes, feeling her muscles loosening in the intense heat. It took only moments to fend off the chill of her descent…

"Focus!" the monk shouted.

Tera jerked, blinking her eyes and looking up. She sat cross-legged on the ground. Her arms had fallen again, the weight of the pots in her hands too much for her to hold for so long. The back of her hands rested on the ground, long white fingers wrapped up the sides of each pot to maintain grip, but loose. She had fallen asleep.

"Tera!" the monk called. He shivered as she leveled her sapphire eyes on him but growled. "To meditate is not to sleep! You must remain focused! Always, always focused! A slip and you do not know what you are capable of!"

"Focus," she whispered, nodding. Despite her arms aching from an hour of meditation (that is what the monk's called holding the pots in the air), she lifted her arms again, gritting her teeth. Leveling them when she could stare ahead at the base of each pot, she let her eyes slide half-closed and began muttering the mantra she'd been reciting before she'd fallen asleep. *"Om mani padmi om…"* The drone became a singular sound, her mind focused on the opening and closing of her mouth. The repetition becoming mindless, her thoughts began to wander…

"FOCUS!" This time, the shout was accompanied by the stinging slap of a teaching rod as it clapped down on her forearms. It might have hurt, had it not hit one of the scaled ridges that rode down either forearm. As it was, it merely served to bring her back aware.

The sun had gone down. She'd been at this since just after lunch…

"Apologies," she whispered.

It mattered not that she had been doing this all day, or that the day before she had been crouched, the same pots balanced on her knees for the same amount of time. The monks bade her do whatever and she was quick to comply.

It was, after all, her redemption.

When it was over, she would put the pots in their place in the shed and follow them to the dining hall, where she would eat rice and whatever piece of meat was being served for the day, along with a small salad of steamed vegetables. If she was lucky, it would be topped off with a sesame seed cookie wrapped with a thin strip of *nori*. After that, she would take a hot bath and have perhaps an hour to read the sutras of the Venerables before lights out.

The monk shook his head. "Tera, you cannot be so easily swayed from your focus. Demons will sense this failure and take you. You will be prey for them, drawn into the path of destruction!"

Without moving anything else, she bowed her head, acknowledging the warning. "Yes, Master."

"The pots are not heavy," said the monk, repeating what he had told her yesterday in the late hours of the day, and every day before that. "Your muscles are not tired. Your mind is not weak.

"You are focused. Focused!"

She jerked awake, having fallen asleep in the heat of the water for who knew how long. Her body was suffused with heat, but this was not the same as the nightmare. Steam rose and she remembered where she was.

"Apologies, Master," she whispered, looking around. Her muscles were weak once more, but not from fatigue. The heat of the water had delivered her into soporific relaxation and her limbs were slow to respond. Just as she began to smile at the odd memory she'd just been reliving, she saw the stone statues of the Venerables across the pool, their sword and palm held before them, glaring…

At her.

She blinked and they were lost in a cowl of vapor that floated across them before reappearing, their eyes staring into the distance.

Stunned, she stared for another long moment before her body began to respond. Standing, she moved toward the entrance, to climb out and dry off.

For a moment, she dreaded the climb back to the temple. Her muscles were so tired…

Prior generations of priests had built the wooden floors that surrounded the pools where petitioners would bathe. These too, were polished to a brilliant sheen. Even through the vapors of the sauna pools, Tera could see the glow of the moon reflecting from the wood. She crawled out of the water and lay on the hardwood floor, feeling every crack and crevice in the slats as her body melded to them.

"I am water," she murmured. She felt as if she had been poured across the platform, ready to drip and drizzle into the dark spaces beneath.

"You will be attacked. Your mind will flow like liquid as they assault your very being. You will feel flames where there are none as they attempt to crawl into your body. They will attempt to bribe you with lies, lead you into traps of your own making. They will try to undo everything you are and you will become as nothing…"

She sat in the central temple, studying beneath the Chief Inquisitor as he taught her about the reality of demons and their ways. He was an old man, with a large wart on one side of his nose and long ears, drooping with age. He had travelled the length and breadth of Minkai during his youth, fighting and exorcising demons as he went. There was no one more knowledgeable about the dangers of demons than he.

"They will lead you down paths of thought so as to make you doubt yourself and your courage. They will have you question everything you are and know. And they will be right, in some cases. At least, for you."

She had stared at him then, with her cerulean eyes, discomfiting to most but with no noticeable effect on her high master. He had seen worse, he told her. "At least you are pleasant to look upon," he said. "You should be grateful."

She knew he was right. She had been told stories of some of the demons she might have to face. Creatures of awful countenance, images of inanimate objects with eyes and mouths that did not belong, beings who defied description, monsters that took the form of human but with orifices in the wrong place and limbs that came from anywhere they wished…

They wore the shape of nightmare. And she had been born of their blood.

"You will learn the sutras until you can chant them in your sleep," he told her when she first arrived. "You will tone and exercise your body until you can accomplish feats that no mortal should be able to. For you are no mere mortal. You have the blood of demons in your veins, but also that of humans. You will be more.

You will think more. You will feel more. You will accomplish greater things than a mere mortal can."

"Yes, Master," she had replied, bowing her head until it touched the tatami. Her long horns had dug into the straw mats and she had ripped a jagged chunk out when she rose. It was the last time she was allowed to offer *dogeza*.

"We cannot have you destroying the floors every time you prostrate yourself," her master said with a flat smile.

He moved to kneel before her and took her by the chin. His dark eyes met her crystal blue and held them for longer than she was comfortable. It felt as if he peered directly into her soul. "You have a good soul," he had said quietly. "You mean what you say and you do your exercises well.

"You are consistent in your training, and that is a good thing. But you have a weakness to their kind, just as they do to you.

"If you do not listen... If you do not learn... you will be lost to them just as easily as they can be lost to you!

"Be strong! Gird your loins for battle. Strengthen your thews! You cannot be weak.

"EVER."

And yet, you are...

She jerked at the thought and tried to move, but her muscles were too done in by the heat and her prolonged submersion. She blinked and stared into the mists above her, seeing eyes that stared back. Eyes that looked familiar, yet foreboding...

Weak... Pathetic... A pretend being pretending to be something you are not...

Fear struck. She had let her guard down. She was alone, both mentally and physically unprepared. The demon had sensed as much.

The truth will set you free...

The eyes seemed to blink, flickering out of existence before returning in a blaze of brilliance. The heat seeping through her body became an intense fire, sweeping through her muscles, tensing and releasing until she was convulsing on the wooden slats, her ridged elbows digging craters into the polished surface, horns tearing long lengths of shredded wood away and eroding the fine work. Her claws dug into the surface, ripping chunks out as her muscles spasmed.

"Get… away… from me…" she uttered, jaw clenching and unclenching such that she nearly swallowed her own tongue.

Puppet…

Doll…

Toy…

The eyes flickered in the mist above her, twisting in such a way that she somehow knew it was smiling, though she could not see its face.

Trinket…

Bauble…

Plaything…

"I am NOT…" she managed.

Ironic pleasure filled its next words. *Are you not? You cringe at their commands. You go where they say. You do what they tell you to do…*

Are you not a puppet, drawn by its strings to where its owner tells it to go?

"No!" She felt the faintest lessening of the spasms wracking her body as she reclaimed her will.

Even now, you are pushed and pulled, a being at the end of the strings…

Strings being pulled…

She jerked suddenly, biting her cheek so hard that she drew blood. A heel slammed into the boards and cracked the wood before sticking. The muscles continued to twitch as she realized she was pinned to the wood. Her heel had grown a spike and driven itself through. An elbow scraped her all-too-human side and drew a red gash before twitching away. Fire flared throughout her body as the demon fought for control.

Strings I control… Not you…

"My body, perhaps," she managed. "But not my mind…"

I do not need… nay… want…your mind…

Images flickered through her then, of fire and smoke. The temple on fire. Of blood pooling on tatami, the heads of the monks lying separate from their bodies, blood seeping through the wooden boards, across her elongated, bloodied talons…

"NEVER…"

Her head slammed into the boards and the sky went dark, sparkling with stars. She embraced the pain, reminding herself that it was HER body that felt it; that the muscles that drew tight and then loosened were her own. Arching her back, she felt her horns dig through the floor boards, drawing up long trails of peeling wood, the years of polish disintegrating before their preternaturally sharp tips. She felt the pressure in her skull and neck. Felt her spine arch to take on the weight as her entire body lifted off the ground.

"MY body…" she whispered, the words grating between clenched teeth.

Trinket…

Curiosity…

Trifle without a name…

Her body slammed back to the wood. The impact rang throughout her flesh, rippling through her musculature, jarring her teeth. She bit her cheek again, felt blood flow from the cut in her side, felt her arm clench and an elbow spike punch between her ribs; another horn that should not be there.

"I… have… a… name!"

Yes… It whispered gleefully… *Temple…*
"Temple Guardian" is your name…
A thing! Not a being! Not a person! A title!
You are…
Nothing…
But a title…

"I am a person!" she gritted out, feeling her body slam to the sides. Each time her sharpened elbows dug in painfully. With each impact, with each trickle of blood, she felt her own body rebelling against her, trying to do as the demon compelled.

Foolish, deluded child…
Alone and unprepared…
Not even your symbol will save you… Where is your piece of silver? Your armor against your own kind? What will you do… alone… and helpless… being with no name?
A title…
A position…
An action…

A thing.

She felt it then.

Doubt.

Fear.

It slid in on icy threads that flickered throughout and beneath the fire that wrapped her body in its harsh glow. What if it was right? What if she WAS nothing more than a position… Who WAS she anyway? Her first name literally meant 'temple' and her last name was an action… 'to protect'… What if that was all she was to these people? To anyone she met? A representative for the Inquisition…

A tool…

Beyond what she did, who was she, anyway? What did she think, when not doing their bidding? What did she like? Did she have any friends? Did she mean anything?

To anyone?

The spasms of her body faded, though she knew they were still taking place, her body gouging the wood and itself in equal measure.

Still, the pain dulled…

Memories flickered in her mind's eye, images of people she had known, places she had been, villagers she had helped. So many days and nights spent walking the roads of Minkai, only to be rejected at first glance by everyone she came across for her appearance… An appearance that had slain her mother before she was even born. An appearance that decried the profession she claimed.

Demon-hunter.

Member of the Inquisition.

Expunger of darkness.

Creature of the night…

Bearer of claw and horn…

Whose ice white skin and purple limbs, unnaturally blue eyes and red horns announced to all the lineage that she drew upon. An image that frightened and panicked the average being; that had no right to walk the earth with them…

Who claimed to be… nay… pretended to be just like them, knowing she was not…

Tears trickled as she fought to remember a moment… ANY moment… when she had determined her own way… When the demon was wrong about her…

WAS there a moment? Who WAS she, anyway? A temple priestess… *onmyoji*, yes… *miko*, yes… But was there anything ELSE to her?

Who ARE you?

The pain had gone. She was afloat in a sea of nothingness. The cool of the night against her overheated skin was gone. The twinges of pain as the demon fought for control over every muscle and fiber of her being faded into nothing. She stared into the distance, seeing nothing, grief etching her face into a mask of horror as she sought to find herself and found…

Nothing…

Her mind sorted desperate through her memories, seeking meaning, purpose, identity… Self…

What was there of her that the temple priests hadn't made her into?

Who WAS Tera Mamoru? Beneath the layers of sutras, the exercises, the control they had taught her? Beyond the ceremonies and battle stances and mudras, what was she?

Why should anyone care? What difference would it make if she had never existed?

Would anyone even notice if she simply faded from being?

She stopped. Stared into the distance. Saw the lines of pages she'd been forced to memorize as a youth, between the ridiculous training she'd undergone and the simple meals she'd been allowed. Saw the symbols of the religion she'd been raised to revere around her, repeated again and again. The Sage… The Venerables… The sword… Silver and gold and bronze and brass… Paintings of temples… Statues of the holy ones who had gone before…

The Venerables…

One with a palm open, meaning forgiveness and peace…
One with a sword; threatening, but whose countenance called one to practice mindfulness; the ability to see through lies.
Both with hard eyes, threatening the onlooker with reminders of the dangers of falling to the illusion that is life.

Calling them to focus on their own well-being and existence.
Calling them to recognize that ALL beings suffer from the lies of this world and asking... No DEMANDING... that they take up the mantle to protect and guide others, who are all companions in pain until the great cycle ends and begins again...

The eyes...

There was something about the eyes...

She blinked.

She was no longer lying on the slats by the pool. She had climbed the mountain to the temple, stood in the great hall, glaring up at the great bronze statue of the Sage, one hand lifted in welcome, the other in meditation. The red velvet pillows and dark satiny brown of the furnishings were irritating to her senses, too colorful to look upon. The statues of the Venerables looked down from their gated positions, calling upon her to recognize...
To see...

She was naked, burning blood flowing from myriad cuts to skew and hide the silver and gold Inquisitorial blade on her back. A torch in her right hand; she drew it back to throw it at the feet of the great sage, to see the tatami catch, the velvet tassles burn, the wood to alight and crackle and turn into charred black and then dust and ashes…

To bring everything down…

Her body shuddered as if caught up in a grip so great that it could not reply.

"NO!"

The scream poured from her mouth, echoed where it should not have, bounced off the heavy belly of the Sage, off the open mouths of the Venerables, off the ceremonial drum and platform, the brass candelabra, the iron bell… Echoed a thousand times, each time becoming louder until her ears hurt and the roar became inchoate and all was sound.

The room shuddered around her, flickered in and out of existence as the demon realized it had not yet secured complete control. She roared forth from the prison it had constructed around her, deep within her own mind.

"Lies!" she screamed into the maelstrom. "Illusions!"

Truth! The demon spat back at her. *A truth you are unwilling to bear!*

"Wrong!" she shouted back. "I accepted this truth when I accepted the path! I am Tera Mamoru, Protector of the Temple!

"That is my being!

"That is who I am!

"That is WHAT I am!

"I am that, and that is me!"

That is NOTHING! screamed the demon, eyes appearing in the swirling light and noise that was all she could make out of the room she knew to be standing in. *YOU ARE NOTHING!*

"But I AM!" she cried back, her voice tiny against the whorl of reality spinning about her. She brought to mind the long days, the passing of seasons as she studied in the temple, the smiles her masters gave her when she accomplished some feat or another.

She remembered the smiles of the villagers she helped. The thanks they sent her way. The blessings they poured on her for her help and care. She remembered the nights praying before corrupted temples, fighting demons of lust and hate and anger and fear.

She remembered the days walking in the sunshine, smiling at the flowers on the side of the road as she wandered, never sure where she was going, but knowing she would be needed at some point for the one thing only she could do.

“The temple!” she cried into the maelstrom. “The sutras! The training! The trust they have in me! THAT is what I am! I AM Tera Mamoru!”

She remembered the trust the people and priests of the land put in her once they realized who and what she was.

She was not what she appeared and that was her strength. As well as weakness. But it was a weakness she had long come to terms with, and the demon could not hold that against her for long.

“And YOU.

“ARE.

“NOT.

“ME!”

You have no meaning! The demon shrieked.

The whirl of light and sound began to abate, the temple hall appearing in front of her once more. Three terrified priests stood in the doorway to the back halls, staring in fear at her as she stood, frozen with a torch in her hand in this most holy of holies, shrieking in voices that were not her own as she battled a spirit they could not even see.

"YOU are my meaning!" she shouted, eyes pinned on the sword-wielding Venerable in his place beside the Sage.

NO!

The power that had overwhelmed her in the baths was fading. She could hear fear in the demon's voice. She still bled from a myriad of cuts, but something felt off. She could feel a difference in shape and form.

Her body had hardened all around into a dark purple, ridged version of herself. As the demon retreated and she grew stronger, her carapace-covered form turned white and supple once more, the arbitrarily-formed ridges becoming human once more and very, very naked.

Their eyes widened as they realized and they turned away, not in fear, but in recognition. The demon hunter was at war with a demon and she was winning. Until it was done, however, they would look away. The temptations of evil were simply too strong.

They relied upon her and her teachings to save them from the apocalypse that threatened them all.

The very recognition of that fact gave her strength.

She remembered the words of a village elder, spoken after the battle to release her daughter from a demon after she was raped and murdered in front of a temple.

The words he had said…

"You are a blessing in the form of a demon."

A blessing…

"I AM," she said strongly, denying the demon's earlier words. "They see me. I am.

"WHAT I am is who I am. That is a demon hunter. A hero to the common man. An expunger of evil, wherever it shows itself.

"I exist to defeat YOU. THAT is who I am.

"YOUR ENEMY."

It cannot be… the demon said in surprise. *You were gone! You were done! I HAD YOU!*

"Beware the lies," she whispered, the room coming into focus with a final snap as its control broke. The wind rampaging throughout the open space was coming from the opened door behind her. Her skin was as cold as the snow and ice it looked like. Her white hair whipped about as she turned to close the sliding door and tie it back into place.

She tossed the torch into the snow outside. It disappeared into a snow bank and went out.

"A lie you told yourself," she replied. "And now… I HAVE YOU."

Closing the door sealed off the elements; closed off the demon in the very chamber it had sought to destroy.

Its howl was unearthly. It shook the rafters. The statues of the Venerables rattled in their places.

Without a moment to think, before the demon could react, she dropped to a lotus position, hands forming the mudras of exorcism and control. The droning sutra, now a well-known companion instead of torturous ally to unfriendly masters and impossible hours of physical torture, forced the demon now into the small part of her mind into which it had forced her.

It fought, gouging her psychic being, causing additional damage to her already scarred and bleeding body. New cuts appeared in her pale skin.

But it could not resist the sutras. Slowly, its being was crushed and compacted to fit into the tiny place it had prepared for her.

And then, she removed that space, and the demon was gone.

She fell back onto the tatami of the Great Hall, legs uncoiling as the last of the demon's vestige faded, little more than an oily black puff in the mental mindscape she had designed for it. Her eyes closed and she felt her body as her own once again, the cool air sending ripples of goose bumps across her exposed form.
She was exhausted. Both body and mind had been hurt by the demonic incursion.
Who she was, what she was.
Where she was…
"Beneath the lies," she recalled the Inquisition Master saying, "is a thread of truth. That truth is what will undo those who are not prepared. From that truth, it will spin a reality that is merely fractions different from the one you know, but equally possible, and equally true, given the circumstances it describes… Demons will lurk and get to know their victim before striking if possible. A demon of lust will follow one who cannot control their urges before striking with a lie that could be the truth… A demon of anger will await the moment when that passion is too strong and then push it just that much

further, claiming their victim in the moment they falter or step too far over the line to return…

"A demon of the mind will pry open your greatest secrets and worst fears and expose them to you, showing you a reality that you refuse to acknowledge for fear of what it means. They will then use that fear to claim you for their own… AS their own…

"Do you understand?"

"Yes, Master," she whispered, smiling at the Venerable that had warned her before the demon's attack. The eyes… She recognized the eyes of the demon from that moment in the pool, glaring at her, gathering its strength before it struck. "I understand…"

In the morning, the priests found her there, still unclothed, sharp black claws folded carefully across her stomach to avoid damaging the tatami. Her head was tilted just so in order to keep her horns from gouging the floor. She was still nude, and they covered her as quickly as they could with a trio of warm blankets after feeling the cold emanating from her snow white skin. They sat and uttered sutras of grace and protection until she awoke around noon.

They fed her a nourishing soup filled with meat and potatoes and carrots, seasoned with the best they could find. They heaped rice on a plate and served her as if she were a visiting saint, thanking her repeatedly for what she had done. They knew that, without her ability to resist, any of them might have fallen victim to the creature she had fought.

And they did not have the training she had.

Outside, the snow fell in deep drifts. In the bath area, it melted as fast as it landed. It was days before anyone discovered the extent of damage done by the demon's assault.

"I will repair it," said Tera. "If you will let me."

"In the spring," said the head priest, smiling at her. "When the snows are lessened, if there is no need for you elsewhere... Then, we will decide if you will repair anything." They had gone about their business, cleaning and repairing the floor of the temple hall, wiping the floors as generations of monks had prior. They went about their business as if nothing had happened, though the evidence was plainly seen.

"You do not fear me for losing control?"

“Everyone fights their demons,” the head priest said after a moment. “Yours, you must fight a little more physically. You won.

“In the end, that is all that matters.”

The Deed Box

by

Victoria Day

“I believe,” said my friend Jenkins “that Townsend will tell you the tale, but you must not ask him to.”

“Oh?” said I as we handed in our sticks and hats to Barnstable, the head doorman at Grey’s Club. “And why might that be?”

“Because,” answered Jenkins, “if you ask him he will certainly not tell. That is …” he faltered “.. That is he will not tell if he thinks you will mock or …”
He stopped as we entered the plush, comfortable smoking room of the club, wherein a few men, both old and young, were scattered about in the deep armchairs. Silently, and with only a small movement of his hand he indicated a chair, pushed close to the fire, in which I could see a tall, youngish man seated. As we drew closer, I could see that he was aged about thirty-

five, had wavy, corn coloured hair, pale blue eyes and wore smart evening dress and a friendly expression. He stood up as we approached, and, transferring his cigar to his left hand, shook Jenkins' hand warmly.

"Jenkins! My good fellow, how marvellous to see you, really marvellous." "Townsend! My dear chap" said Jenkins " Allow me to introduce my partner in the firm- Arthur Russell!"

"Russell- glad to meet you, sir! Any friend of Jenkins' is mine too!"

"Thank you Mr Townsend", said I, really quite cheered by his frank and kindly greeting.

"Well, well, Jenkins- what brings you here on this filthy, cold night?"

"Oh, well, we have just dined at Guiglioro's and came in for a night cap", laughed Jenkins. "We are celebrating our new partnership- Jenkins, Russell and Jenkins, Solicitors at law!"

"Ha!" said Townsend "then you shall have one- Brown!" he roared, waking up a few of the older gentlemen from their naps, "Brown! Three brandies!"

As we awaited the arrival of the brandies, I glanced around the Club room. I had only just been made a member and had yet to have a good look at the place. It was much like any other such London Club- with a warm, cushioned atmosphere, plenty of comfortable leather chairs, tobacco smoke, huge fires in this raw season and elderly lawyers- for this was a club exclusively for those connected with the Law. I had enjoyed a modest, but fruitful career since I had left Oxford, most of that due to joining the firm of Jenkins and Jenkins six years ago. My Jenkins was the younger partner- the older Jenkins being his father. Jenkins Senior was still Senior Partner, the idea being that, in a few years time his son would take over. My elevation to Partner was exceedingly gratifying, although I think I may not be accused of boastfulness if I say that my First in Law and my diligence, as well as my easy way with difficult clients, were assets to father and son!

When the brandies arrived we all settled back in our chairs and I extended my toes to the fire.

None of us spoke for a few moments. Jenkins cast a few looks in my direction, the purpose of which was for me to be quiet. I obeyed, and after a minute or so we were rewarded.

“ Hmmm,” mused Townsend, “hmmm- new partners.. in a solicitors’ firm”. I was about to speak, but there was a flashed look from Jenkins- this, evidently, was business.

He settled himself further into his chair, relit his cigar and began.

“About eleven years ago, when I had not been down from Cambridge long, I joined the firm of Robinson and Parker. They were a very old firm of solicitors, located in The Strand. Sadly, they are no longer there, but that is another story. My interest was, and still is, in property law, and I soon found that this was an area in which I could really be useful to the firm. In that I was happily correct as, after two years with the firm, I was made a partner. One morning I was summoned into Mr Robinson’s office and on entering the room was rather shocked to discover him standing, with his hands resting heavily upon the back of his chair, his face grey and damp looking. Shocked, because I had never, in the two years I had worked there, seen him appear anything less than smartly and severely dressed and very much master of himself.

"'Townsend- good chap,' he began, 'be so good as to sit down. I – I am sorry to appear thus before you, but I have had something of a shock'.

"He stopped, wavered on his feet and, if I had not sprung forward to catch him and seat him gently down he would have, I believe, fallen to the floor. I loosened his collar a little more- strange to say that it was already somewhat untidy- and pressed a glass of brandy to his lips. He grasped it with quaking hands, as I stood back marvelling that such a staid old gentleman should now look so frightened. For there was no doubt to my eye that the man was almost scared out of his wits.

""Townsend- my dear fellow, thanks. I have had a terrible shock, but I asked you here to take on a rather special trust"

"I was, as you might imagine, gratified by this, but also puzzled. However, I was young and somewhat adventurously inclined- perhaps more than a solicitor should be- and longed to hear what had brought on this behaviour in my employer.

“”Please sit, my boy, please sit and I will explain”, evidently the brandy was doing its work as he seemed to be gaining a little more composure.

“”Townsend, you have not been with us long, but I see in you a man of integrity, a careful and a loyal man.” You may be sure that at this point I wondered what on earth was coming. He continued.

“”Townsend, what I am going to tell you may seem to you odd, bizarre even, but every word of it is the truth. And believe me, my dear boy, I would not burden you with it unless it were not absolutely necessary.” I sat and prepared to listen.

“”Many years ago, this firm took over the business of a rival firm, Langdon’s. The transaction was not, alas a happy one. James Langdon was, to put it bluntly, a brute. How the man ever managed to qualify as a solicitor was and is a mystery to me. He was ill mannered, brusque and quite bereft of the social graces. Besides which, there were stories, which I shall not go into here, of cruelty to his wife.”

“Here Mr Robinson mopped his brow and seemed again to have paled.

“”But, whatever his social shortcomings may have been he had a secretive and close nature, sly some

would say, and because of that he attracted the business of some unscrupulous clients. I must say in defence of our firm, that most of these were not taken over by us; I myself insisted on it. One day, the day before the legal transference was to take place, Langdon himself came into this office. I won't bore you with the details, Townsend, but the upshot was that there was one client he had neglected to inform me of."
"Here again, Mr Robinson pressed his handkerchief to his brow and passed it round the back of his neck. He gulped- yes gulped at the brandy before he continued.
""I still think to this day that the man tricked me- he had never mentioned this client before, or what... what he had entrusted to Langdon. It was this."

"Mr Robinson then slowly, wearily drew from his waistcoat, the most singular set of keys I had ever seen. Instead of a metal ring they were held together by a plait of hair- golden hair, it seemed, but somehow dusty and odd looking. For some reason I could not bring myself to look at it, it seemed in some way nasty . Mr Robinson too, appeared unwilling to touch it and held the set by the largest key. This was a huge thing; fat and heavy looking, far too big for the deed box he reached down from the shelf behind his desk. With a sigh, he placed it carefully on the desk, paused and inserted the large key into one keyhole and turned it. He then selected another delicate silver key and turned that in a second keyhole. He opened the lid and took out a smaller box, a dull grey coloured metal one. This, with the utmost delicacy, almost with loving care, he settled next to the larger one. He then sat down heavily and spoke.

“” This is the deed box of Langdon’s last client. As I have previously mentioned, the facts surrounding this are odd, and you may choose to believe me or not as you will. But- I believe what Langdon told me that day, I must.”

“I stayed silent as there seemed more to come.

““From the moment I accepted this deed box, I have never been easy in my mind, and it is with heaviness in my heart that I ask you to accept the guardianship of it. Please know, Townsend, that if you refuse to accept, I will in no way judge you the worse for it. I do not lightly ask it, nor do I expect that you will agree. For in this box, there is a woman’s soul.”

"I stared at Mr Robinson and then the box. My next instinct was to laugh, but the next second this impulse died. I cleared my throat.

""A soul? A human soul? Sir, I.."

""Be assured Townsend that what I say is nothing less than the absolute truth. I know because I have seen it."

Silence fell.

""And what do you wish me to do sir?"

"" I am an old man, and have today received discouraging news about my health," he raised a shaking hand to quiet me, " I must ask you, and heartily wish I did not have to, to assume the guardianship of this box and its contents."

"Well", went on Townsend, "you may call me the most abject fool, but I repeat that I was young, ripe for an adventure and, besides I did not believe him!"

He sank back into his chair, and said in a thin voice, "I do now. I agreed to take over guardianship of this particular deed box, which required me merely to sign the appropriate papers. As soon as this had been done Mr Robinson's mood seemed lighter and then, only then, did I feel that I had, perhaps made a mistake. For he seemed suddenly pleased to be getting rid of it, and

I am sure that he shuddered at having to touch it again as he passed it to me; marked difference to his previous caressing of it. However, despite Mr Robinson's sudden dislike of touching the box, I gladly took it in my hands. To me the tracery of the metal felt somehow thrilling to my fingers. I stroked it and it felt, ridiculous as it sounds, warm to the touch.

“” One word, Townsend,” said Mr Robinson, “ be careful to keep the metal box locked in the large box and, do not touch it too much.” This did not seem to make much sense, and I thought that the old chap's brains must be weakening- as I said I did not believe any of his story- souls in boxes! Dashed nonsense!

“Part of the conditions of my guardianship was to take personal possession of the deed box, and to this end I locked it in the patent safe in my rooms. That night I went to place the deed boxes in it. I was annoyed when the larger one would not fit in the safe. I was forced to take out the metal box and put that in on its own. As I did so I felt an irresistible urge to stroke the box again- really it was a beautiful, if oddly decorated thing- the tracery was not skilfully etched, but somehow I could not but gaze at it. I shook myself, locked the safe and I said to myself, “Balderdash” before settling down to my supper. About half an hour later, my friend Ames called, and we decided that we would just pop along to the club- this club- for a nightcap. Imagine my disbelief when, upon my approaching my usual chair, there upon it was the smaller of the two deed boxes. I started at that, choked a little on my brandy, but then decided that it must be merely a double. It seemed, however to be of the same shape, size and design as my deed box. I peered closer, and for some reason felt compelled to touch it. The next moment though, it was swept off the chair and plumped down unceremoniously by Ames on the side table.

“” Urgh,” said he, “what in the world is in that box, whose is it? It’s uncommonly heavy for such a thing- a deed box, eh! Yours is it?”
“”I’m not sure whose it is,” I said “that is, it’s not mine!” I did not say these words particularly loudly, but it seemed that there was a sudden strange silence in the room, a chill-stopping of noise rather than a shocked reaction from the rather docile company. The stillness came from the box, it seemed to me, rather than from the men. Ames too, did not react with any undue

interest. The only one affected by my words was the box itself. I took another mouthful of brandy, lit my cigar and sat down. I tried my best to attend to Ames as he told me what he had been up to recently, but all the while my eyes strayed to the grey metal box. After an hour of this, in which the box did not perform any further tricks, I made my excuses to Ames, and headed home, in my haste and distress leaving the box behind. I did not realise this until I was near home, and by that time the club would have been locked up for the night. Very well, I said to myself, if it is the box it will be safe until tomorrow and if it is a double mine is safe at home. You can be sure that the first thing I did when I entered my rooms was to fling open the safe, as I must know what was happening. I could not believe what I saw- the box sat there, undisturbed! I sat with my head in my hands, in dreadful confusion but slowly convinced myself that the box in the club, although of a similar rare design was, after all a duplicate.

"I turned the deed box in my hands, trying to compare this genuine one to that it the club, but my memory seemed strangely fogged, and I seemed unable to recall exact details of the club box. The other must be a double as Ames had said it was heavy, but this one felt pleasantly light in my hands. It seemed warm and soft to my touch, more like velvet than cold metal. I felt the most powerful urge to open it, but being so tired, I locked it up in the safe, and retired to my bed. I often think how lucky that immense tiredness was. I wonder what would have happened had I opened it then. Thank God I did not.

“The next morning, there were no signs of boxes where they oughtn’t to be. I checked of course and it was in the safe. I set off to our offices with a relatively light heart. It was the beginning of spring and a warmer breeze was heralding a change in the weather. Upon entering my own office and hanging up my hat, I turned to my desk. My heart seemed to jolt and stop. A deed box, the exact – do not mistake me- the exact box sat there on the desk. I goggled at it- until interrupted by my clerk, Harris. He burst in with that morning’s correspondence in his hand.

“” Good morning Sir! I did knock, but I took it that no one was here, as you didn’t answer. My apologies, Sir!” He was on the verge of leaving with the papers still in his hands, but remembering himself, he put them on the desk. His hand must have touched the deed box.

“” Yah! Oh what’s that, sir?” he yelped as he drew back his hand. “ Sir- it, it hurt me!” We stared at each other- he with regret at his panicked reaction- I with a growing sense of horror and realisation.

“” It’s not mine , “ I managed to splutter out. No sooner had I said these words than there was, as before a peculiar stillness- more of atmosphere and mood than of sound or movement. It is hard to explain such an out of the way feeling as I had then, and I hope to God that I never have it again. It was as if something dead had spoken to me. Harris chattered on, ignoring my now grey face and sweaty brow. I caught a glimpse of myself in the mirror behind my desk- I looked exactly as Mr Robinson had looked on the day I agreed to take over as guardian of the deed box.

“How I got through that day I shall never know. I shivered at having to touch it. I examined it for as long as I could bear the almost sensuous feel of it- just enough to make sure that it was the very same box. I placed on its top left corner a spot of sealing wax- it is a purple wax, one which is used for my private correspondence- there is no other like it, and to make assurance doubly sure, I marked it with my initials. Then I placed it in my office safe and locked it carefully, taking my keys, as usual, home with me I could hardly wait to get home to check on the contents of the safe, and yet was dreading what I would find. If the box were not there- how could it have got to the office? If it were there.. I dared not think how it had got back. For there was now, in my mind no doubt that this deed box was always the same one, and for some reason, known only to itself it wished to keep me close.

" The disgust, horror and disbelief I felt when the deed box sat before me, on my dressing room table, with purple wax in the top left corner and marked with my initials almost overwhelmed me. I believe I was close to fainting. I clutched my hands to my face and moaned like an animal. I remembered no more until my landlady, Mrs Kerr found me the next morning. I had not reported to work and Mr Robinson had evidently been concerned. They lifted me onto the bed and attempted to prise my hands from my face and straighten my legs. This being achieved I was nursed by Mrs Kerr for a week, before I could even open my eyes. A few days later, I began to come to myself and Mr Robinson was summoned. I'm rather afraid that on seeing him I attempted to attack him- luckily being so weak I only shouted out “You! You!” Between them they calmed me and Mr Robinson sat beside me.

“” Townsend, I deserve everything at your hands. I have sat here all night, and I know from your unconscious words what has been happening, and what you have seen. I beg you to forgive me, I had no choice. I told you what the box contained, but I knew that you did not believe me. I must, for both our sakes, tell you the whole story.

“” Langdon had, as I said, a client about whom he had neglected to tell me when I refused to take on his more unsavoury customers. I berated him for this, as it would seem that, legally I was now obliged to take him on. The man had deliberately tricked me, and for the moment I could do nothing. He merely laughed in my face and told me that try as I might I would never be able to get rid of this person. The story he told was this- that some twenty years before a man and his wife, she no longer young, but still handsome, had come to his offices as he was about to leave. Their demand- for such it was, they would brook no refusal - was that he draw up their wills there and then. Knowing Langdon I have no doubt that a great deal of money was involved. He admitted them to his office and began the task himself, as his clerk had gone home hours before. He thought that this would be a simple job, but as they began to talk, he knew that this was very far from being the case. The couple were not young, but were, it seems devoted to one another. Unhealthily so, according to Langdon- at the time I brushed this off- he was hardly the man to be a judge of love and devotion! As the man went on though, it seemed that what he wanted from Langdon was most unusual. He and his wife were, he said, not to be parted even in death, and whichever of them were to die first, the other would bring to Langdon a metal box containing the soul of the other. Langdon was to be guardian of both boxes and pass that trust on to another if he could no longer fulfil the terms. Langdon admitted that at the time he could scarcely stop himself laughing, but that their money was as good as anyone's and they could put in what they liked- legally he could hardly be made responsible for the impossible! Or so he thought. After seven years the wife died, and one evening, again as he was shutting his office, the man appeared carrying with him a grey, etched box. Langdon, still not taking all this seriously, took the box and assured the man that he would honour his trust. Accordingly he locked it up in a second box provided by the man, with the two odd keys you have seen. The man then insisted that these three keys be bound together in a plaited lock of his wife's hair. Langdon admits that on touching this hair he felt a curious tingling and warmth in his fingers. When the man had left he felt also the most powerful urge to touch the box and caress it. This then led onto a desire to open the box in which the woman's soul supposedly resided. Veering between disbelief and curiosity, he opened the box. He refused point blank to tell me what he saw, but said that he would give all he had not to have seen it. Also- he seemed curiously averse to touching it once the guardianship had passed to me. You can imagine then my jumble of feeling after he had told me this- he had passed on this guardianship and so could wash his hands of the whole thing- I alas, could not.

"" The years passed until the day I asked you to be its guardian. I wished you to take over more of the property and will business of the firm, and saw no reason why this ought not to be passed to your care. I myself had not taken Langdon seriously and so had no qualms about you accepting the term which seemed harmless, if a little eccentric. Shortly before you were due in my office, I decided that I would take a look in the box myself. As soon as I touched the box I felt the most peculiar twitching in my fingertips. It spread up my hands and into my arms. I can only describe it as exactly the feeling I had when I first held my newly married wife in my arms when we were at last alone. The most wonderful, yet frightening feeling of love, desire and fear. Then, just as Langdon had described the unrelenting pull of the need to open the box….I succumbed to it also.."

"" I waited," said Townsend, now sitting up in his chair and fixing us with his eye as if to dare us to mock. " I waited, but he did not tell me what he saw, despite my pleas.

""No," said Mr Robinson, "I will never tell another living soul- not a living one. You are a young man and have suffered much. I do not think that either the man or his wife intended to harm others or to frighten them- like many in love, they were foolish and selfish. It was a terrible thing for me to pass on the guardianship to you, knowing what was in that box, but I hoped that like me, you would not take it seriously and so would not be curious enough to touch the box- alas, it had other ideas. I am most profoundly sorry. I believe that which you have experienced, which neither I nor Langdon did, the incidents of the box following you. I believe that is what has happened- can be explained, if one accepts the strangeness of all this. The box began to follow you to keep near you. It could only bear the touch of the guardian- that is why others were repelled by it and the guardian so attracted to it- it must keep itself safe. I believe that the soul of the woman sensed that her husband was ill. He died this morning. When you feel strong, we must take the box to – (here Mr Robinson named a place that I may not divulge) and complete this business."

"So, said Townsend, that is what we did. We completed all requirements laid down by the will, and both souls- if you believe it- are together and at peace .So, luckily am I."

There was a long silence- Townsend had at last told his tale.

The Field

By Jessica Oeffler

Lying on her back, she watches a star shooting across the space between the branches above her, *Make a wish,* she thinks to herself. She is alone, listening to the night sounds around her, watching the stars twinkle, allowing her mind to be blank. She is at peace, lost in the bliss of nature, when nature becomes silent. Everything around her falls deadly quiet, she is no longer alone. A stillness falls over the area, a presence of something unnatural. Sitting up, trying her best to keep her breathing normal, she looks around the clearing, for something out of place, something which does not belong, the unnatural thing which has come upon her.

Seeking, searching, her eyes scan the area, *There,* she sees a shadow among the shadows, an area of darkness out of place in the shadows, a vague humanoid shape, seeming to watch her. No longer feeling safe, she stands, gathers her things, and starts to walk with her back toward the figure. *Show no fear, don't look back,* she repeats in her head like a mantra, but she keeps her eyes on the ground all the same, afraid to raise her head, to see the fate which awaits her.

A rustling noise in front of her causes her to raise her head in alarm. *How did it move so fast?,* she thinks to herself, catching her breath, trying to still her racing heart. The figure from the shadows is now in front of her. Standing just inside the clearing, definitely a humanoid figure, male, wearing dark jeans, and a black hoodie, with the hood pulled up over his face. She can't see any details of his features, but his eyes seem to shine, reflecting the dim light of the moon and dancing with it in the darkness. *That's not possible,* she turns quickly, head down again, back toward the figure in the hood, walking faster. She is scared now, sweat slicks down her back, her heart pounds a rhythm in her ears, her breath gasps in and out of her throat.

She once again hears the rustling noise, but this time, it almost sounds like tearing fabric, terrified, she looks up. *Oh, gods, please, no, how is this happening?,* once again, the hooded figure has come around to where she is facing. *I don't understand, how can anything human move so quickly?* Keeping her eyes up this time, she turns back the way she came from. A small scream escapes her throat. *No, oh gods, please, what are they?*

As she spins helplessly in a circle, her things falling from her suddenly loose grasp, she feels real terror for the first time. Surrounding her in a circle in every direction she could possibly run, is a hooded figure with reflections of moonlight dancing in the eye sockets. *How did I not notice them? Where did they come from?*

Frozen in fear, unable to move, she stands and stares at the one in front of her. As one, the hooded figures reach up with gloved hands, grab the front of their hoods and lower them to the nape of their necks. A scream rips from her throat as she sees what was hidden beneath, not reflected moonlight, *fire, where their eyes should be, nothing but skulls, no flesh, no eyes, just skulls with flames where the eyes should be.* Wicked fangs, razor blade sharp, reflected the starlight in the skulls' lipless grins. The hooded figures close in on her, taking off their gloves to reveal hooked claws where fingers should have been, the fire in their eyes dancing maniacally. Realizing, too late, she will never again see the light of day, she collapses to her knees, and does the only thing she can think to do. She prays to her gods to be saved but it seems as though her prayers are falling on deaf ears. The skull faced demons descend on her.

At first, she feels every bite, every tear made in her flesh, and she cries out in pain, over and over again, praying still to her gods to be saved from this fate. Feeling death creep over her mind, she closes her eyes, a feeling of numbness washes over. Then, a feeling of feather-lightness comes over her, she opens her eyes.

She is watching the demons tear into her flesh from above, growing farther and farther away from her death, she is being pulled upward, and it is glorious.

For the first time, she feels a true sense of peace within.

-fin-

The Ghost Snake.

James S. Malheiros

The truck carrying Mr Abraham's cattle stopped right in front of his house. The cowboys delivered the beasts and arranged them in the lot, cow by cow.

It was one more day on Gustavo Mayer street.

In my house, I was trying to arrange the books and magazines on the shelf. It was almost lunchtime and my stomach was angry. But never mind.

It was one more day of the nineteen-eighties, and things couldn't have been more shaken up than they were.

But it was a Saturday and my family wasn't working at that time. Saturday was time to watch television in the morning and for me to play by the house. I was a kid then but already knew about the story of the family, what we wanted from this life and what it meant to us.

George Hilton was dealing with some wires and technical things in the house. Sandro Jarbas was reading one more of those books of horror that he had bought in the famous Blumenau bookstore, The Centerbook. Mama was cooking lunch when it happened.

The creature started to move in the roof, the creature that used to control our minds at that time. When a red truck came by the road and crushed a big snake that was crossing the street. Mister Abraham and the cowboys saw everything.

-The truck made some damage.- said Mister Abraham, looking at the smashed corpse of the big snake.

-Let's take her out of the street.- said one of the cowboys.

And together they put the body of the snake by the side of the road.

The snake lay there, dead, smashed, waiting for the insects to come and eat her, but that wasn't what happened. Lunchtime came, everybody ate. The Saturday passed away, with the sound of the birds around, and nobody paid attention to the dead snake that was lying beside the road in front of my house. The night came and something strange started to happen.

It was the beginning of one more night, when a strange light could be seen, in front of my house, close to the ditch. The climate was fresh, and what happened was fantastic.

The body of the dead snake started to glow brightly with a strange light and she started to shine all around. Then, a misty image of her body, like a ghostly reflection, floated over her and disappeared straight away into the darkness beneath the house. The crushed body of the same snake still lay there, on the ground, dead.

Inside the house now, everybody was watching television, waiting for the time to go to bed.

The night passed, silently, and soon it was another morning.

I woke up, ate my breakfast; coffee with milk and bread with schmier, that stuff we put on the bread to eat in these parts, and went straight to the hall to play with my toys in the garden. It was another Sunday.

I played the entire morning.

But something was wrong in the street, now the snake was decomposing beside the road but her soul had disappeared.

One more lunch was to come, and then came the evening.

George was picking some boxes to put electronic pieces inside, he was in Mama's room, I'd been arranging my toys and now was putting all of them

inside a big bag when it happened. I climbed up on the sofa to close the window, when George screamed.
-Watch out!-
I looked forward and saw the snake, preparing to strike me.
I hurriedly closed the window, pushing her out.
Was it the dead snake, that had come back to life and was haunting us?
After closing the window I never once saw the same snake again.
-All right with you?- George asked me, sweating because of the heat of that day in the town, the small town of Blumenau.
-Yes, it's all right.- I said but I was scared.
I never again saw a snake in Blumenau but her ghost was in the corners while we lived there. We eventually left Gustavo Mayer street, but that image of the snake never left my mind. Sometimes I think can see her by the street, just by the corn plantation when I go for a ride with my mother. Now we live in the big city, and my search for fame selling stories to magazines has increased my struggle to be a writer. I sincerely feel lost, lost in work writing, lost in my life, having learned hard lessons in my life, now here I am, struggling to be

a writer and to survive. Still, don't have money, I choose to live with my family, to stay with my brothers, still living with Mama. I just love them. I guess I'll never leave them.

I never again saw the ghost snake, and hope never more to see it.

Perhaps she's lost, between Blumenau and Curitiba, just waiting to come catch me someday. But if this day comes, I'll be ready to face her.

The Milk

By Amanda Phoenix

Randall Holmes awoke to the sound of the alarm. This day was not particularly different than any other. His preparations included a shower and shave, the gathering of his things into a backpack, and a quick sip of stale coffee before heading out the door for his daily walk.

He was a short lump of a man, five foot four and not particularly good with confrontation. He was retired at fifty-six and living off a meager pension that he acquired from various jobs of little significance. For extra money, he taught school as a substitute. It was an irregular work schedule that allowed him to still have a lot of free time during the week to do what he pleased. Most would have found this arrangement suitable for a single male his age, it did provide for his needs, but he would have rather had steady employment and steady company. He managed to stave away the "only the lonely" blues by keeping a strict schedule of events, only switching things up when he received more work that week from the teaching gig.

He volunteered for after school academics on Mondays, had Toastmaster meetings on Tuesdays, and finished the routine with the church on Wednesdays and Sundays. It wasn't perfect but it provided enough company to keep him from being a hermit-crab that retreated into its shell in accepted defeat. His rounds in the neighborhood allowed him to talk up various clerks and shop attendants, making casual conversation like old friends.

Every day was the same. First, he stopped at his favorite comic book store, a gourmet coffee house, the library and then sometimes shopping for groceries, if he only needed a few things, otherwise it was the bus and home again for the day. Randall did not expect things to change. They never did. So you'd think that someone, anyone, would have noticed when things began to divert from the small town scheme of things. It wasn't a grandiose change at first, but a subtle one.

That morning, like any other morning on his free days, Randall rounded the corner of the street toward the comic book store. A plain white van was parked on the corner. "That's new," Randall thought, "I hope their restroom is not out of order. I might need it." As he entered the small store, bells announced his arrival. He immediately began picking out his favorites, but then noticed something strange. There was a tingle in the air, a feeling that something wasn't quite right. He looked around and paced nervously. "Where is everyone? Hello back there, I'm ready to check out." Randall put his books on the counter and walked around the room. "Maybe the new teenager that works here forgot to lock up last night and no one is in yet." He said out loud, hoping that someone would hear his insolent complaining. There was no answer. For Randall, it was a personal affront to his daily routine. He mumbled hateful insults under his breath and then stormed out of the store, leaving the comic books on the counter.

Feeling extremely put upon, he continued on to his favorite coffee shop. It was not very large but at least they had gourmet coffee, or at least as gourmet as a small town can manage. He walked through the front door to meet a smiling young barista and matched her smile with one of his own.

"There was no one at the comic book store this morning. I can't believe some young people today- no responsibility. It started me off on the wrong foot, but your smile has made my day, miss. I am glad to see a bright ray of sunshine. What do you recommend this morning? I want something special."

"I can't recommend much that has regular milk or cream. I'm vegan and I don't drink milk but the coconut milk latte is delicious. I recommend two pumps of vanilla. It gets me going in the morning."

"It just so happens that I'm lactose intolerant. That sounds delightful, miss. I'll have that."

"Coming right up," She said with an enthusiastic smile. Randall put his hands in his pockets and rocked back on his heels. He let the smell of the fresh grounds fill his nostrils as he began to relax.

"This is just what I needed," He said to himself. When the barista handed him the cup, he gave her a grateful nod and a smile. "Thank you so much, miss. I can't begin to tell you how much you've cheered me. I hope you have a good day today too." He sat down at the table by the window so the glow of morning light could filter in on him as he cradled the cup in his arthritic hands. The warmth felt soothing and good going down with each measured sip. He sat there and watched the customers come and go. He noticed a chatty woman with a robust physique saunter in. She was squeezed into a pair of sweats that hugged her rather large curves.

"I'll have a regular latte with skim milk, two shots of espresso, a shot of mocha, three pumps of vanilla and half a shot of hazelnut if you don't mind… Oh.. don’t forget the extra foam. I have been trying to cut down. I am on this new diet and things haven't been going well. I should have seen some progress by now. You know how things are..." She continued to rattle on in a vexatious tone, the shrill sound of her voice echoing harshly in Randal's ears. He cringed, curling his shoulders inward in defense.

"I wish she would shut up. How rude and obnoxious can a person get." Randall thought. He sat there with his cradled cup and watched as she took a big gulp of her latte. Her expression and her posture immediately changed. She became stiff and robot-like. The organic swirl of her hips was gone. She stopped talking. When the barista asked her if everything was ok, she didn't answer. She looked blankly ahead, put her cup down on the counter and walked out without saying a word. Randall looked over at the bewildered barista.

"I feel that I must apologize for her. Some people are just so rude. Don't let her ruin your day." Randall said.

"Oh, that's ok. I am used to it. As a matter of fact, that's the third person this morning to have that reaction. It can't be the beans. I roasted them last night and I know they weren't burned. The people who have ordered the coconut milk have not reacted that way. There could be something wrong with the regular milk. It could be spoiled and they just didn't want to say anything." The barista explained.

" I guess you could be right. I can't drink milk but I can taste it for you and see since you're vegan. All I need is a sip. A small sip won't hurt."

"Thank you. That is very kind of you." She handed him a small coffee cup with a few sips of milk at the bottom. He turned up the cup and drank it down.

"Augh. It has a metallic aftertaste. I can barely taste it but maybe it is ruined. I wouldn't sell any more of that miss."

"I was afraid of that. I wish someone would have said something. I could have fixed the problem sooner. I will have to go in the back and get a fresh jug. My distributor is bringing me a new brand of milk. That could be it as well. Maybe it is a cheaper brand and you can taste the added vitamins. Oh well. Not every day can be shiny I guess."

Randall nodded in agreement. While the barista disappeared into the back room, he sat and watched outside the window, waiting for her to return. While he sat in the haze of his inner thoughts, a disturbance erupted outside. The woman that he had seen earlier with the robust figure was chasing someone down the street. She appeared to have an expression that looked quite rabid. Her nostrils were flared and her eyes wide.

"Lover's quarrel." He said out loud. Randall chuckled to himself at the sight of the woman in the tight sweats running down main street with her large haunches jiggling as she ran. When he had finished his coffee, he saw the barista come in from the back room.

"Goodbye, miss. I hope to see you again tomorrow." She gave the same warm smile and waved as he headed out the door. Randall was feeling quite chipper now. He was ready to go to the local library to check his email on the library computer and check out some books until he saw a plain white van zoom past. “I can’t believe how fast people drive these days! I’m glad I wasn’t on the street yet. That van could have clipped me. Don’t they know that it’s 35 miles per hour in town? He must have been doing at least 60.” Randall fumed.

On his walk down main street Randall passed a rather tall man that had a wild look about him. Randall could feel the man's presence without looking back over his shoulder. He felt the man’s predatory eyes lock on as he passed. Suddenly the tall man ran after him and then lunged forward. Another man, squat and broad, leapt seemingly from out of nowhere onto the tall man and began ripping at his flesh moments before the tall man's attempted leap at Randall. Randall did not wait to see what would ensue but he could have sworn that the squat and broad man was gnawing at the tall man's ankles as he looked briefly over his shoulder. Randall ran all the way down Main Street and did not stop until he made it to the library doors. He raced inside, his heart pounding and his head dizzy from overexertion. Randall leaned on the counter, out of breath. "I almost got mugged!" Randall declared excitedly in the direction of the librarian.

"Oh my! Are you ok?" The librarian asked, putting her hand up to cover her mouth in shocked disbelief.

"Barely," Randall said. "There was another man that stepped in to fight him off but I didn't stay to see how that would turn out. I hate violence. I wish I could have said thank you, but my rescuer seemed pretty angry with the man that jumped me. Maybe they had a spat before my near altercation. That would explain the behavior... not that I don't appreciate it but ... it just seemed odd."

"Well. You are lucky. You barely made it here by the skin of your teeth. Sounds like things could have been a lot worse." The librarian said.

"You may be right. I'm grateful that I'm ok and to be breathing normal again... but I am not sure if this old ticker could take much more." Randall said placing a hand over his heart.

"Why don't you get a free cup of tea? We have decaffeinated varieties. It's a new thing we're trying. It could calm your nerves." The librarian suggested.

"What an excellent idea. Thank you. I will do that and you should be careful when you lock up here. There are dangerous persons on the loose."

"I will. Thank you."

Just as Randall turned to go to the library computer room, he saw a toddler in a stroller. Randall loved children. They did not seem to have the horrible qualities that some grown-up people had. They were hopeful and innocent, always looking at life through a positive lens. He walked over to the mother, who had grabbed a carton of milk from her diaper bag. The label said 'friendlies'. She opened the carton, began pouring it into a sippy cup and then handed it to the child who began supping it fiercely.

"My what a lovely child..." Randall began. But no sooner than the words had fallen from his lips, the child began snarling at him and gnashing its small teeth.

"Anna that's not nice. She has never reacted like this I promise." The mother whimpered as she tried to restrain the child. The child began attacking the mother with her nails as the flustered parent tried her best to gain control.

"She must be tired. I have heard that small children can be difficult to handle if it's near bedtime." Randall said to the embarrassed mother, who blushed hard and continued to try to calm the child as he backed away slowly.

Randall checked his email quickly and decided against the books for now. He felt suddenly tired and irritable. "Maybe after all that has happened today, I need a nap." He thought. He didn't bother with the bus, deciding to walk the rest of the way to the grocery store for some lactose-free milk and then hurry home. It was just his luck. The grocery store was out of lactose-free milk. "This is just great!" Randall fumed. The only available milk was regular friendlies'. Randall felt entirely put upon now. "I can't do without milk. I guess I will have pains in my gut tonight. I really do need some sleep." He sighed to himself. He reluctantly picked up a half-gallon of friendlies' brand whole milk and stepped up to the cashier. As he waited in line, he eyed a bag of cookies on the impulse purchase rack near the cash register. He grabbed the cookies and slung them down. The cashier gave him a reproachful look but did not say a word. "I'm sorry that I'm so cross. I don't mean to be. I was almost mugged today and nothing has gone right. It has been a horrible day. I don't mean to take it out on you." Randall said apologetically.

The cashier gave him a weak "That's ok." and handed him the change.

"Wow, I really do need that nap," Randall said to himself as he went out the grocery double doors and headed home. He continued looking here and there to make sure he was not being followed by the crazy tall man who had tried to attack him earlier. When he had made it to the apartment complex, he finally felt like he could relax. It was quiet, eerily so, but Randall did not seem to notice. He turned the key and went inside making sure to lock the door behind him. He got out the cookies and poured a glass of milk. "I will treat myself to a snack before I lay down for my nap." He said allowed. He dunked his cookies as he did when he was younger, a fond bit of nostalgia from his youth that always made him feel warm all over. When he was finished with the cookies he gulped the milk while it was still cold. He drank it so fast that he didn't notice the metallic taste until most of the milk was gone. "Augh! That milk was spoiled. I can't believe it!" He yelled. Then suddenly the room began to spin. He felt violent and angry and he didn't know why. He wanted to rip someone apart. He felt a lust for blood that he couldn't comprehend. Randall threw his empty glass against the wall. It shattered. He slammed the kitchen chair against the floor until it smashed into bits and pieces all over. He made his way to the door. He clawed at the door not remembering how to open it. He snarled and clawed at the air. He began kicking and banging at the door. Drool slipped from his lips and began to puddle on the floor. He felt rabid and couldn't think. His thoughts felt like white noise that pierced his ears. Everything felt too loud. He yelled at the top of his lungs and howled in pain. Then suddenly the door burst in on him, knocking him to the ground. As he lay there on the floor in an incoherent daze, Randall saw men in white. Their heads were covered in some sort of mask. The white noise blared even louder in his head. He suddenly sprang up. He wanted to kill these new intruders. He wanted to bite into their necks and make them bleed. He let out another snarling howl. Just as he began to lunge, the pain hit him in the neck. His neck was on fire. A poisonous burning filled him. Everything blurred and swirled to black.

In the apartment parking lot, a man in a black suit stepped out of a plain white van. He had peppered gray hair and a red silk tie. He approached the apartment complex and entered through Randall's door. "Is the situation under control?" He enquired with an air of authority to one of the four men wearing white isolation suits.

"Yes, sir." Answered the man holding the tranquilizer gun. "He's already under, Mr. Jones.

"This is specimen 237." One of the men added.

"Don't forget to check the fridge." Mr. Jones interjected.

"Yeah. He has friendlies'. Looks like he drank quite a bit." Another man in white said.

“Bag this one up and throw him in the van with the others." Mr. Jones said.

"How many more towns will we need?" One of the men asked.

"At least several more. I have a list of the towns that received the friendlies' brand. We can compare the results from the ones that we have chosen to be the control group of this experiment." Mr. Jones said. "The big man should be very pleased with our results. We should be able to weaponize soon." Mr. Jones added.

"How do we know that this won't get out?" One of the men asked.

"We take our time and eliminate any witnesses. You wouldn't believe how many gas explosions get out of control. Besides, not many people would believe it if the truth did get out. " Mr. Jones explained.

The men in white chuckled at this as if they were laughing at a harmless childhood prank. One patted his neighbor on the back as he gave the thumbs-up sign to signal their mission was a success. They all loaded up their specimen, one Randall Holmes, into a white unmarked van and sped away.

The Old Girls

by Trev Hill

The Old Girls

The door opened creakily and she saw the large, hall-like classroom, filled with lines of silent students seated with their backs to her. The creaking of the door made them turn their heads towards her, gazing apprehensively, with a mixture of curiosity and a hint of malicious mirth, although some faces had an air of woe and sympathy.

She stood, uncomfortably, shifting from one foot to another, awkward and self-conscious under the intense stares of her new classmates. The silence grew, echoing in her ears until…

A voice boomed out,

“Well? Is there a reason you have disturbed us, young lady?”

She gasped under the direct question and stammered a squeaky response…

"I… I…."

"An aye-aye is a Madagascan tree-dwelling mammal, which I don't think you are. Unless you're speaking German, in which case I don't think you resemble a pair of eggs either… So, shall we try again?"

She coughed slightly, her throat dry from embarrassment,

"Ellen Porton… I was told to come here"

"Ellen Porton?"

"Yes, Ellen Porton..."

"Ellen Porton...Sir!"

"Yes Sir, Sorry, Sir... Ellen Porton, Sir!"

The silent sniggering of the other girls echoed from their eyes. Ellen felt hot, a single drop of sweat snaking down her back, making her squirm.

"Better! So you have manners of a sort. You may also address me as Mr Hastur… Well, don't just stand there wasting our time… take your seat."

"Where should I sit?… Sir?"

"You have eyes, don't you? Find your place… it is waiting for you, it has been since the last occupant made way for you."

Seeing an empty chair, she moved slowly towards it, her cheeks burning under the glaring scrutiny of both her classmates and Mr Hastur's malevolent gaze, which seemed to be drilling into the top of her bowed head. Receiving no further guidance or correction, she pulled out the chair and sat down.

"Good, Miss Porton, You have learned your place… now be sure to remember it… Everyone else knows their place, don't you class?"

Ellen jumped in surprise as the class stood as one and chanted out "Yes Sir, we do!" before being motioned to sit by the darkly-smiling teacher.

"Good. You see Porton, everyone knows their place in my class… if they don't they soon learn… and they are sure to be reminded if they forget."

*

Ellen sat down on her bed. She was alone in her small, bleak cell. Even at the end of the day, she was isolated. Students… inmates.. of this school, The Malebranche School for Correction, were not expected to keep company, they were expected to gain correction. That was why she had been sent here, after all.

The class had dragged on. Mr Hastur was probably the strictest teacher she had ever seen. No, no 'probably' about it… he *was* the strictest, hardest and, to be honest, the scariest person she'd ever seen. It seemed even the other people in the class thought so. She had quickly learned that each person kept one eye on their work and another on him. Even when everyone had their heads down, slaving over whatever exercises they had to do, Ellen could see the shoulders tensing as Hastur passed nearby. Occasionally he would stop… and stand… and do... nothing, but whoever he was next to seemed to shrink into themselves more the longer he was by them.

At one moment, Ellen lost sight of him, peering around to her left, she felt his wooden pointer slide under her chin, softly but snakelike, and his hissing voice in her ear,

“Looking for something, Miss Porton?”
The pointer rose, and she was compelled to stand… up… upright… the end of the pointer lifting her onto tiptoe… she could feel the eyes of the class somehow swiveling to watch her, even though their heads stayed down. “While you are here, you work, and only work, Miss Porton, unless I tell you otherwise or I speak to you. Is that clear?” The pressing of the pointer under her chin stopped her voice, Hastur’s hiss turned into a slight growl, “I said, ‘Is that clear?’”. She tried to nod but the pointer pressed hard into her throat. She whimpered a “Yes!” “Yes… what?”
“Yes… Sir!”

"That's right, now sit down… Next time, I might not ask so nicely."

*

The classes were long, strict and, for the most part, silent. Mr Hastur's voice boomed when he was telling them something. That was alright… It was when his voice was quiet you had to worry, a sinister hiss, like the escape of compressed malevolence. Ellen could tell that nobody would be punished in this class… because everyone was too terrified to do anything wrong… but would that be enough for Mr Hastur?

*

Even when the class was dismissed, they rose and filed out of the room silently, heads down, then hurried off to wherever they were meant to be, nobody spoke to her, even looked at her… even that was too much.

Dinner, she sat alone, avoided. The others still watched her beneath lowered gazes, heads down, a position she learned quickly to adopt…

*

Before the meal began, the prayers were being said. Hastur walked amongst them, their shoulders rising and tensing as he passed. Although she couldn't see him, she felt his presence. The tension crept up her spine, she glanced to the side. Hastur's hand shot out and caught her by the top of her hair. He slowly raised his arm, pulling Ellen onto her feet, just as he had raised her with the pointer… only this time he pulled her from her place, her chair crashing to the floor, and walked the girl, running on her tiptoes, down the aisle between the tables to the great table at the top. Reaching the table, he waited for one of the other teachers to bring a chair. And a bowl. Ellen stared dumbly as Hastur poured the contents of the bowl on the chair… dried peas. She moved her eyes towards him as he held her, vice-like, by the hair, his face next to hers.

"Don't look at me, girl!" he hissed. She snapped her eyes forward, although they kept trying to watch him. He eased her toward the chair. "Hands on the back of the chair." Shaking hands crept out and seized the backrest... "That's right… now… kneel." Her eyes moved, uncomprehending, to the side… "DON'T LOOK AT ME… KNEEL!" She paused… "Hold your skirt…

that's right… now lift it up above your knees… higher… now… KNEEL… ON… THE… CHAIR!" Slowly, she moved her knees onto the chair, onto the hard, dried peas. Wincing, she tried to pull back only to hear his growling voice once more order her, "KNEEL!" The jabbing pain of the peas pressed into her joints. Despite her best efforts, she let out a squeal as her weight pushed down, forcing the hard little balls, like needles, into her skin. His hand was pressing the back of her knees, her calves. She whimpered, her hands clenching, white-knuckled, the backrest of the chair.

"Now, you shall say your prayers there, loudly, so we can all hear… and you shall stay there while the others eat… This is your place, I told you… You WILL learn your place!"

That night she shuddered in her bed, remembering the needle-like pain of the grains in her knees and the hidden eyes staring at her, half-sorrowing but also with a suppressed glee that it was not one of them. New girls, she had quickly learned, were targets.

Ellen lay in the cold darkness, her clenched hands hugging the thin, coarse blanket around her. The silence was punctuated only by the occasional footsteps of a teacher or warden along the corridor but somehow, the stillness itself seemed loud, noisy, as if it was not silence, but a sound in itself… a sound which kept her awake. Eventually, she began to make out the sounds of other girls whispering…

*

As the days went on, Ellen learned new things, secret thing: how to see without being seen, how to watch without looking and how to hear without listening. The other girls had ways of communicating, this much she had realized, but she had not worked these out. What seemed worse was that she wasn't being allowed to find out. She felt that she was being tested, observed… assessed.

It was one day, towards the end of a particularly gruelling grammar class, Ellen's hand was aching from writing conjugations. She stopped writing to flex her hand when she heard it. She frowned and moved her head to the side, only to receive a stinging slap to her face,

“Who told you to stop writing?” Hastur growled. Panicking, she picked up her pen and resumed the task. “Don’t let yourself be distracted, Miss Porton,” he crooned, in an almost hypnotic, melodious way, looking thoughtfully around. There is only one thing worse than letting yourself be distracted, and that is…” he purred, looking slowly around with a wolfish sneer, “… being the one who distracts… especially when I know who they are.”

Ellen sensed the tightening of the atmosphere and the angry buzz amidst the silence.

*

Across the dining room, Ellen saw her; the blonde girl, hair cut to shoulder length, a weakened hard expression and a stiff movement which she did not normally have. As she sat at a nearby table, their eyes didn’t meet. Ellen knew. The problem was, she didn’t know how to but the other girl was obviously aware of it. Ellen was, however, aware of the rumbling discontent being voiced around the silent room.

"I'm sorry!" she thought.

"Idiot, be more careful!"

She wasn't sure whether the blonde girl had said this or, if someone else, which of them it was being said to.

"You could have been caught!"

"She needs to learn! She needs to know!"

"Says who?"

"They are watching her…"

*

That night the whispering was louder. Ellen buried her head beneath the pillow…

"She can hear!"

"She always could."

"But now she knows…"

"Then we can start…"

*

Ellen was washing before bed when the voice cut through her thoughts.

"You have to learn." the blonde girl said, without speaking.

"But how?" Ellen whispered. The girl's eyes flashed angrily without looking at her.

"DON'T SPEAK!" she snapped, wordlessly. "And never react! That was what you did wrong today, now he suspects."

"Was it him who hurt you?"

"No, the others… They aren't ready to let you in yet but you need to know."

"Know what?"

"Don't ask questions, just learn!"

"But how, I don't know…"

"What do you think you're doing now? Just don't listen to everything… not everything you hear is us."

A sharp whistle shot across the conversation and the blonde girl picked up her things and left, quickly.

*

The empty chair announced itself to the class the next day. Hardened unlooking eyes, expressions tightened, saw and yet… nobody seemed surprised.

"That was you…" came the new voice. Ellen didn't see the dark-haired girl who wasn't talking to her. "Now you know, learn!"

"Was it you?" Ellen asked.

"No…"

"Who?"

"You'll learn…"

*

"It's her own fault! She shouldn't have told you!" came the whisper.

"Her own fault"

"You'll have to learn now, there's no going back!"

"No going back!"

"Yes, you'll have to listen…"

"Listen!"

"There will be a new one soon… Say nothing…"

"Say nothing!"

"Nothing"

Ellen sat up, drenched in sweat, yet shivering in the cold cell. The voices had woken her, or had they? Had she been awake? What struck her was that this was the first time they had communicated directly to her. She shivered and turned over to sleep.

*

The following day the classroom door creaked and a new girl entered, much as Ellen had some weeks before.

"Say nothing!"

"Don't make the same mistake… they are watching you!"

"He suspects already!"

"You're the reason she is here…"

The pointer slammed across the new girl's table as Hastur welcomed her.

*

"What happened to her?" Ellen asked.

"Don't ask!"

"Don't!"

"But the new girl…"

"How do you think you got here?"

"… the empty chair?"

"She wasn't the first…"

"You weren't the first…"

She was puzzled. When the other girls communicated it was when they were together, in the same room, yet somehow these communications were in her cell.

Perhaps some of the older girls, those who had been there longer, were able to communicate further…

"Who are you?"

"No names"

"No names"

"But, do I know you?"

"You will…"

"Yes, you will…"

*

Hastur walked around the class, as usual. The new girl had already had her initiation to the school several days before. The pointer repeatedly whipping across her hands whilst she stood in front of the class. Ellen had received hissed warnings to do and communicate nothing, someone else would choose the time, if there was one. Now she knew what it had been she felt on her first day…

It was Hastur's custom to suddenly pounce on one of the girls without warning, find a fault and either humiliate them or dish out some physical punishment. It didn't seem to matter how serious or even real the offence was, it just seemed to be a technique for keeping them in fear. Ellen realized he was walking along the back row of the class.

"It's your turn!" the dark-haired girl warned her.

"Watch out!" giggled someone else. Ellen froze, confused, just in time to realize Hastur was behind her.

"Stand up!" he ordered, his stiletto voice penetrating her spine. She rose quickly, staring straight ahead, knowing better than to look him in the face. "Recite the lesson!"

Ellen paused, struggling to grasp what he had demanded of her. "Recite… word for word, what you have just written!" he ordered. She fumbled around mentally, trying desperately to coordinate her thoughts…. "The lesson, Miss Porton… now!" She opened her mouth…stammered and choked… no words came out. She could hear everyone, everyone, some sniggers, some consolations…

"So, not paying attention, idling away and not learning… Hands!"

"But, Sir… I…"

"Don't argue with him!" Came an urgent warning!

"So, you want to argue, Miss Porton… Arguing gets you more… HANDS!"

She put her hands out over the desk and stared straight ahead and the pointer swished downwards, cracking across her palms… and again…

*

The girls stretched up, then to the side. The exercise class, as with all others, was done in silence. No team games, no games of any kind, just stretching, running and individual gym work, as a group. They raised their hands up and stood, stretched, holding the posture.

"How are your hands?"

"How do you think?" Ellen replied.

"It was your turn," came another

"It might not have been if you hadn't distracted me!"

"Oh, it was… it was your turn."

"Even if you had recited, he'd have found some reason, you should know that by now,"

"How did you know it was my turn?"

"You mean you haven't worked that out yet? Thought you were smart."

The exercise mistress stopped near them and the conversation paused. She favoured them with a longer than usual stare… The girls bent forward to touch their toes. She made them hold the position slightly longer than usual as she walked slowly in front of them. Up into a high stretch…

"Do you think she heard?" Ellen asked.

"We wouldn't be here now if she had! Probably suspects…"

"Oh come on, they all know, anyway…"

"Yeah, but it's different if they catch us, you know that!"

"Did they catch the other girl?"

"Maybe, but she made it obvious. They don't take chances. She wasn't the first, nor will you be."

"Me?"

"All of us… someday."

*

A week later, the girl with the dark, short hair had left an empty chair and so the cycle began again.

*

"Count his rhythms, that's how you know!"

"Learn his paths"

"His paths?"

"Where he goes, when he does, who he chooses…"

"He doesn't 'chose', he's already chosen.

"But it looks so random, you mean he has patterns?"

"Unless you give him a reason…

But then, he will always find one…"

"That's how she knew? Did you know, too?"

"Hahahahah…. Of course…."

"We knew…."

"Well thanks for telling me, I thought you were my friends!"

"He would have still chosen you."

"But it was fun to watch…"

"It's always fun to watch…"

"It wasn't fun for me!"

"Don't you enjoy it when someone else gets chosen?"

"Knowing it's not you?"

"NO! It's horrible… I don't know how you can say that?"

"Learn to…"

"Yes, you should learn to…"

*

As the days past, she learned his movements. Who would be chosen, when it was her turn… sometimes, even who would disappear. The conversations with her classmates became more frequent and with the others at night…

"You were wrong today!'

"Wrong?"

"Never wrong!"

"You said it was my turn… it wasn't, he chose the girl to my left!"

"Not wrong…"

"Never warned you!"

"But some of you did, as the class was starting…"

"Not us!"

"no…"

“But you knew?”

“Knew”

“Always know!”

“You knew he’d change his mind?”

“Didn’t…”

“He didn’t!”

“Your time is coming…”

“So, he will choose me another day?”

“He has already chosen you…”

“Already…”

“So, will it be the hands again? Or does he have punishment patterns?”

“Not that…”

“Chosen the other way…”

“What other way?”

“Can’t tell…”

“You don’t know?”

"Know, always know…"

"Can't tell… but always know!"

"So when?"

"Soon…"

"Must go… he's coming…"

*

"Where do they go?" she asked the girl.

"What?"

"When they go, where?"

"Not here! Never here, never ask!"

"How do you speak through the walls?"

"What?"

"I can speak with you, but only when you speak to me, is that it?"

"Don't be stupid… nobody can speak through walls!"

"Then how do you do it… if not you, who?"

"You're wrong, it's none of us!"

*

Ellen felt his presence. She was alone in the dark… unable to work out where… somewhere. She couldn't see him but felt him…

Suddenly, beside her, was the blonde girl who had originally contacted her. She was different… she was not just dressed in white… she was all white… like a… ghost.

“Not everyone is us!” she said, spoke, like a normal person.

“I don’t know what you mean!” Ellen replied, speaking as normal. “Where are you now?”

“Everywhere… they are everywhere…!”

“Who? The teachers?”

A hissing sound slowly grew around them. The blonde girl looked terrified, she started jumping, staring left and right… the noise increased.

“Must go, they know…”

“Always know!” came a voice within the hiss.

“Who? Wait…!” The hiss increased. The girl became to whine, moving backwards. Ellen’s hands reached out as the white figure slid away… She made a final grab to hold the white shape but felt nothing…

Emptiness...

Then the hands seized her…

"HANDS, MISS PORTON… HANDS!"

She woke up, drenched with sweat.

*

"Why don't you show yourselves to me during the day?"

"Can't… just watch!"

"Fun to watch…"

"Always fun to watch!"

"Who are you?"

"Don't ask…"

"Never ask!"

"Tell me… are you in my class?"

"Everywhere…"

"Are you… teachers?"

The voices giggled….

"Hahaha! No…, not teachers!"

"Never teachers…!"

"So, you're girls… like me?"

"Girls… yes…"

"Like me?"

"No… not like you…"

"Older…"

"Much older…"

"So that's why? You've been here longer…"

"Much longer…"

"So how long have you 'Old Girls' been here?"

"Always… here!"

"Yes… Old Girls have always been here!"

"How can you talk through walls? The girl in class said…."

"Not through walls… nobody can talk through walls"

"That's what she said… None of the girls can do it!"

"Old girls… "

"Old girls can talk everywhere"

"Old girls are everywhere…"

"How do I learn to do it?"

"Only Old Girls can do it…"

"Only if you become one… of us…"

How do I become one…?"

"Don't ask… never ask!"

"You are chosen…"

"Or, you can choose…"

"Choose what?"

"Choose to come to us…"

"It will be fun…"

*

The exercise class was finishing. The teacher dismissed the girls to the washroom. Ellen moved nearer to the girl. She began washing.

"Where are they?" she asked.

"What? What are you asking about now?"

"Which class are they in? Are they a separate group, or what?"

"Who? What are you on about? We shouldn't communicate here, it's dangerous…"

"The other girls, the older group?"

"You're mad, there are no other girls?"

"Yes, there are, the older group…"

"There aren't there is no older grou…" She stopped, staring at Ellen, her face becoming a slow picture of comprehension and then a mask of fear… no, terror.

"No, don't talk of them… why are you talking of them… " the girl whispered aloud… "Why? Are you talking to them? Don't talk to them…" she began to babble, faster and faster.

"The Old Girls… they said…" Ellen began.

"Stay away from me… Don't talk to me!" the girl screamed. The others stopped and stared. Nobody ever spoke aloud. The teachers came in, seizing the screaming girl, dragging her away as she shrieked at Ellen, "Stay away… you can't… you can't be one of us…!"

The other girls stood, staring at Ellen, expressionless faces of fear and loathing. Then they dropped their gaze as Hastur slowly walked amongst them, picking up the girl's dropped towel.

"Well, Miss Porton… what are we to do?"

*

"He knows…"

"It is too late…"

"You were already chosen…"

"Now he knows…"

"What can I do?"

"You?"

"Nothing… nothing to do…"

"It.. is… late…"

"Help me… can't you help?"

"Help…?

"No!"

"Only watch…"

"Yes, this will be fun to watch"

"But what will happen to me?"

"Can't say…"

"But it will be fun to watch…"

"Tell me what to do…!

The voices changed, they spoke amongst themselves…

"Yes…"

"It would be good!"

"We have an idea"

"Stop him… don't let him…"

"But how…?"

"Kill him first!"

*

The next day she knew was to be her last, it was obvious. At breakfast, nobody sat near her, nobody communicated. Of course the other girl had gone, no word, no explanation… but now, no friends.

Even Hastur had paid her no attention in the class, that in itself a sign that he had plans.

In the exercise class, then the washrooms… alienated… nobody stood near.

Evening meal, she said the prayers, ate the meal and then, as the prayers for the end of the meal were said, she slipped the kitchen knife down her sleeve.

*

"It is time!"

"Time… hurry!"

She rose from her bed and slipped silently from the room… her bare feet moving, soundlessly down the cold, stone corridor… to the wooden stairs. Slowly, painfully slowly, she took each step at a time… No creaks… she mustn't make them creak… his room… his snuffling breath… bestial snores…

"Hurry! No time…"

"Quickly…"

"This will be fun to watch…"

"YEESSSSSSSS!!!!!!!"

*

Back in her room, Ellen collapsed on the bed, shaking, the blood fresh on her hands and clothes. She stared blindly at the dripping knife.

"What now?"

"Now?"

"What should I do? I need to hide the knife…"

The voices sniggered.

"Too late…"

"They know it was you…"

"You left a trail… little drops of blood… all the way home!"

"They are coming for you…"

"Help me! You must!"

'Why 'must'?"

"We didn't do it!"

"But it was your idea!"

"Not ours… we just told you what you were thinking…"

"You wanted to do it!"

"And it was fun, wasn't it? You enjoyed it, didn't you… Feeling the knife cut and the gurgle of his throat…"

"It was fun to watch!"

"No… I didn't!"

Hahaha! Liar!

"Now they are coming for you."

"What will they do to me?"

"Don't ask…"

"Never ask!"

"There must be something I can do… a way out! Please!"

"A way out?"

"A way out… yes… there is a way…"

She could hear the footsteps hurrying down the corridor and the hastening voices of the school staff.

"Become one of us…"

"…an Old Girl!"

"But how?"

"You have to want to…"

"…to join us…"

…join us…"

"It will be fun…"

"But how, how do I do it…?"

"You know…

Yes, you know…

Do what all the Old Girls before you have done…"

Ellen rested the knife on her throat…

"… just as we all have done before…"

She slid the blade downwards, feeling the warmth of the spurting liquid…

The darkness surrounded her as she slipped down… down…

“At last… now I am free from here… free to get out…”
“Free?”
“free… get out?”

“No, never get out… Old Girls are always here… Everywhere… we can never leave…”

*

The door opened creakily and she saw the large, hall-like classroom, filled with lines of silent students seated with their backs to her. The creaking of the door made them turn their heads towards her, gazing a hint of malicious mirth, although some faces, some of which she knew, had an air of woe and sympathy. And each face was of terror, pain etched into the faces of the damned. Red, blank eyes stared at her in recognition, whilst their demonic grins welcomed her…

She stood, uncomfortably, shifting from one foot to another, awkward and self-conscious under the intense stares of her new classmates. The silence grew, echoing in her ears until…

A voice boomed out,

“Welcome, Miss Porton… find your place… you will learn it… even if it takes an eternity… which we have.

A sniggering voice whispered,

“This will be fun to watch!”

THE SPELL

Marquita Martin

Weaving dream spells, hands fluttering
  Like moths in the lamplight.
Your skirts swirling, hair flying,
  My mouth dry with desire.
Sister, have mercy on me.

Music wails around us in the cool dark.
Your body keeps beat to the drums.
My heart keeps beat to you.
Weave your chants around me.

I'd rather be your enemy than nothing at all.
Sister – have mercy on me.

UNTITLED

Marquita Martin

Spinning
  Crushed red velvet
    And gold.

Turning
  Turning in, turning out
Round and round,
  A spinning wheel.

Angels cry and demons sing.
Why did you leave me in this dark dominion?
Dancing under a cold sky?

Spinning,
  Turning in and turning out.
My heart sings, flesh cries,
                    "Hallel".

Up The Dark Lane

Trevor Hill

“We cannot possibly use THAT name!”

“But that is the original name, it’s all part of the history!”

“That might be so, but we’d be shut down in an instant if we tried! Find an acceptable alternative or the project simply won’t go ahead.”

Paul O’Shea left his boss’s office scowling. They’d been planning this project for months and done all the necessary admin and now it all hung on some cursed name which was quite acceptable several centuries ago but now threatened to bring down the wrath of the gods if used before nightfall. Well, they’d face that when they came to it. Meanwhile, time for some serious digging.

O'Shea assembled his crew in the local Prince Rupert Hotel. "The Stalwarts", as he had christened the regular members, were sampling the hostelry's local delights. A little early, he felt, but they knew their work and their limits. Meantime, he was interviewing some new members from the locale, specialists in their fields, he was told. He sipped his coffee, hoping to god that they weren't the usual self-important local bumpkins he normally had to deal with. Thankfully, they weren't too bad, he had to admit, although Dr Bartholomew Bartlett PhD was a trifle annoying. However, as he had the most contacts and some local media status, he was put in charge of the "auxiliaries". Once O'Shea had his troops, he arranged the first briefing for the following evening in the Prince Rupert.

The conference room was abuzz with excitement as the auxiliaries and local trades-folk assembled and wolfed down the complimentary sandwiches and wine.

"Hark at the Hoovers!" a stalwart technician was heard to comment, "All the same on every job, extras, super-luminaries, local specialists… all the same, all bloody hoovers. Come up to the table and hoover it all away!"

His stalwart buddies nodded sagely at his words of wisdom and surveyed the melee whilst hoovering their pints. O'Shea entered the room and the multitudes found their seats.

"Ladies and Gentlemen," O'Shea began, "you're probably aware that there is something special planned in the local area." The multitude chuckled accordingly. "Well, until today I could have told you, but then I'd have had to kill you!" Cue more chuckling. "As you are no doubt aware, myself and my stalwart crew are members of the television production History Hunters, a popular archaeological programme. You've also probably worked out that the History Hunters will be filming an episode in your fair town of Severnsbury. WE are very excited about this, as it is a beautiful, well preserved mediaeval site with a lot of history, but again, you probably know that too."

Nods and chuckles and, "get on with it," sighs.

"Well," O'Shea continued, "now for the moment you've all been waiting for." The multitude pricked up their collective ears. "A few months ago Sunforques, the well-known national pub and hostelry chain, acquired premises in Severnsbury intending to convert the current site into a small mediaeval themed tavern. Naturally, they want to keep the buildings as close as they can to the original state whilst incorporating the structure into the new interior design. However, they have also permitted for archaeological research to be done on the foundations of the building (which is still standing I hasten to add) before proceeding. Of course, we are very excited at this unique chance and also very honoured that History Hunters has been asked to undertake the research. And so, to aid us in our endeavours, we have gathered together several locally respected specialists, that is, your good selves!"

Laughter and applause.

"Neal Tobias, Severnsbury Sentinel. Could you tell us, Mr O'Shea, where the archaeological dig is to take place?"

"Well, Mr Tobias, I was just about to do that but let's say your shrewd, archaeological journalistic technique has unearthed the information," winked O'Shea, to a roar of merriment. "So, in answer to Mr Tobias's digging, we'll reveal that the site is located in the 15th-century structures which form the junction between Fish Row and Grope Lane."

Gasps of excitement and astonishment.

"This area, as you know, is not only one of the oldest and most picturesque areas of the town but also has a long and rich history of trading and..."

"Oh yes indeed!" piped up Dr Bartholomew Barlett PhD. "A special sort of trading indeed, for instance, did you know that the original name of Grope Lane was Grope..."

"Yes, thank you, Dr Bartlett! I'm sure many people will be aware of the colourful past of the area. Ladies and Gentlemen, may I introduce you to Dr Bartholomew Bartlett PhD, who will be leading our team of local researchers?"

Polite applause and Bartlett lovingly waving to all, especially the cameras.

"Now," continued O'Shea, "let's discuss some technical matters, shall we? Then we can excavate the bar!"

Wild applause.

During the post-announcement soiree, O'Shea was making the customary introductions between the new members of the team. Accordingly, he approached Dr Bartlett, accompanied by a woman. "Dr Bartlett, I'd like to introduce Dr Hayley Mackenzie, who'll be working alongside you."

Dr Mackenzie held out her slender hand whilst Bartlett puffed himself up to the required level of pomposity. "Ah DOCTOR Mackenzie!" he declared, holding on to his wine-glass and cigar. "And from which honorable institution do you hold your title?" he asked. Dr Mackenzie smiled slightly, withdrawing her hand.

"The Open University," she replied unselfconsciously. Bartlett's eyebrows rose and fell.

“Oh, my apologies, I had assumed it was from a proper institution, like my own,” He sighed.

“Of course, one would have liked to, Mr Bartlett, but having a job and a family does get in the way a little,” Dr Mackenzie replied tartly. The tone was lost on Bartlett, who shrugged in slimy sympathy,

“I wouldn’t know, Dr Mackenzie, having never married. One devotes all to one’s discipline, you see. Ah well, needs must as the devil drives, I suppose, eh, Mr O’Shea?”

O’Shea had coloured somewhat at Bartlett’s comment,

“Dr Mackenzie comes highly recommended, Dr Bartlett, something supported by some of my fellow OU graduates.” Bartlett nodded with a self-assumed comprehension and not a hint of embarrassment,

“Of course, Mr O’Shea. I understand completely. Well, I shall look forward to working with you, Dr Mackenzie and feel free to drink from my well of experience.” He raised his glass and turned back to his little group.

O'Shea and Dr Mackenzie turned and walked towards the bar.

"Oh god, sorry, Hayley!" O'Shea sighed.

Hayley shrugged, "Heard it before but that line was a killer, wasn't it?"

"What, the 'never-married' one?"

"Yeah, probably never found anyone stupid enough, even from the OU!"

The location of the excavation was a narrow lane in the centre of the town. Severnsbury had been a prosperous town in its heyday, a religious and mercantile centre which attracted many traders and traders. The centre of the old town still retained the classic black and white houses of the 15th century, with their distinctive timberwork and time-sloped structures. Grope Lane led from the more recent renovations of the High Street up to the old mercantile centre and the cobbled street of Fish Row. This would be a particular headache for the excavators because of the need to remove any cobblestones individually and mark them to return in the exact spot from which they came.

O'Shea 's team loved this kind of work. The overtime was amazing. The local research team stood in the lane surveying the relevant buildings.

"Amazing building, isn't it? Nothing fancy as such, but all the history in its little rafters," O'Shea smiled, his more romantic side beginning to peep through. Hayley Mackenzie nodded with a slight smile. One or two of the other researchers ran their hands across the wooden beams on the outside of the houses.

"Our job, " O'Shea began, "is to go down…"

Bartlett chortled, "Very apt, considering what this place was, eh? Did you know, Dr Mackenzie, that the original name was…"

"Yes, thank you, Mr Bartlett, I do know."

“So, who knows what we’ll find, eh!?” Bartlett droned on.

O’Shea continued. “We’ll be trying to get down to the inner foundations and maybe around the outside. It seems the lane was narrowed at some point, might be interesting to find out why and if it had any connection with Dr Bartlett’s original name,” he smiled, nodding at the appreciative Bartlett.

“So what exactly will we be doing, Mr O’Shea?” asked a young man in the group. O’Shea turned to him.

“Now, John… is that right?” the man nodded, “Yes, sorry, John Frenchman every one, assistant archivist at the county libraries. Well, John, you’ll be searching for land records, etc and finding out about the architectural records and so forth, seeing how the buildings changed over the years. Also, maybe some legal records, court documents, etc to see if we can get a few tales of the past, that kind of thing. I’m sure there must be something juicy.”

There were a few knowing smiles from the local historians which set O'Shea's heart aglow.

Several weeks had passed and the digging and filming was due to begin. The crew had set up and the archaeologists were prepping the digging team. The celebrities were doing the rounds and getting to know everyone. The research team had come back with some important details and a few stories, most of them well known. Things seemed to be going to plan, except a problem had arisen with the security staff.

"So what is it? Do they want more money?" O'Shea asked, throwing his hands up in exasperation. "They could just ask!"

"To be honest, Mr O'Shea, I don't really know," admitted the chief of the security team. They either won't tell me or they just say they are never going to stay on this site again. "Pretty vehement, some of them too."

"But are the conditions so bad?"

“Conditions are great, Mr O. The site is pretty secure, no real problems there. It’s warm, dry… just can’t seem to keep some of the guys. Those that have stayed have asked not to have to stay in the building overnight.”

“Oh, this is bloody ridiculous! Is it cold or wet there? Do they want wi-fi, porn channel? What?” O’Shea cursed. The security boss shrugged, mute. “Well try to get some more and throw a couple of tenners in their back pocket if needs be!”

The security boss nodded and left silently. O’Shea gripped his vape between his teeth and muttered a curse that would have driven the devil away in embarrassment. The door opened and Hayley MacKenzie peeped cautiously into the room.

“Trouble Paul?” she asked. O’Shea nodded sternly.

“F-ing exodus of night-watchmen. Can’t keep them and nobody will say why.”

"What did the security chief say?"

"Nothing, but he knows something, I know he does... He's holding something back!"

"Intuition?"

"You don't survive long in my job if you can't tell. Sod it! What's the problem?"

"The problem is..." Mackenzie smiled, "that you need a drink!"

O'Shea nodded. "A big stiff one!"

"Wouldn't mind a big, stiff one myself, as well as a drink." The good Doctor smirked.

O'Shea recoiled in mock-horror. "God, you've been working with Bartlett too long!"

They locked up the office and headed over to the Prince Rupert.

The hotel bar was bursting and O'Shea found the noise and bustle annoying in his current state of mind. He finished his pint and suggested they find somewhere else. Hayley nodded,

"I know just the place, old coaching inn. I think you'll like it."

"Sounds good, what's it called?"

"Errrm, The Coach and Horses, believe it or not."

"Now who'd have thought it?" he chuckled. "You're local?"

"Not really, but it does a great pint of... Somerset apple juice!"

"And I took you to be a shandy girl!"

"Well, why should a girl have ale on the lips when she can get the tongue in cider!"

"Doctor Mackenzie!"

And they went.

The pub was fairly busy but comfortable. The crowd was generally working locals, not a trendy young crowd. Mackenzie and O'Shea found a free table in a corner and O'Shea nipped over to the bar, returning with two bright orange pints of Cheddar cider.

"So," he asked, sitting down and taking a sip, "How's it going with the research team?" Mackenzie took a large sip of her chilled cider and smiled, semi-triumphantly.

"Not bad at all, although Doctor Bart-Bart is a pompous prat!" she answered merrily.

"Yeah, sorry about that but..."

"Ah, no problems, he lets us get on with it. He makes outrageous demands and we ignore him. He's just a blow-hard. WE know OUR jobs."

“I know, it’s just he has access to people in power.”

“Whatever, Paul. Like I said, the research is going OK. Perhaps even more than OK.” She smiled knowingly.

O’Shea rose to the challenge. “Looks like somebody has a secret they are dying to tell me,” he opined, staring into Mackenzie’s smirking face.

The smirk peaked and she took another sip. “Oh yeah! You’ll love this…” she began. However, O’Shea’s loving would have to wait as there was a rather loud story being told across the bar which made both O’Shea and Mackenzie down their glasses and listen.

A stout, middle-aged man was standing at the bar, regaling a group of what appeared to be his drinking buddies. He seemed excited or agitated and the audience appeared transfixed. O’Shea nodded towards the orator.

“He’s actually one of the security team. I think he’s a foreman.”

“Could be worth hearing then,” Mackenzie replied.

They stopped talking and listened.

The tale went on with a few interruptions of bawdy comments or laughs but the tone was generally one of seriousness. One or two of the assembled group nodded knowingly and caught each others’ eyes. Eventually, the teller had told all and there were a few more serious nods, light jokes and the conversation turned to fishing and football. O’Shea waited until the speaker left the group, heading towards the gents, and casually stood up and strolled to the bar.

As the man returned, O’Shea “ stepped alongside him, “Hello George, fancy meeting you here. Is this your local?” he smiled. George’s eyebrows rose and he nodded at O’Shea.

“Oh, alright Mr O’Shea. Enjoying a night out are yeh?”

“Yes, nice place? I’m here with Dr Mackenzie, would you like to join us?”

“Oh, well, very kind of yeh, but…”

“Nonsense, George! I’m sure your friends won’t mind for a minute, what are you having?” O’Shea pressured the security-man, motioning to the barmaid to bring some fresh pints over. George accepted he was taken and shuffled over to the table with O’Shea. He nodded to Mackenzie and sat down, raising his pint to his lips

O’Shea sat down opposite, took a sip of his cider and smiled across at him. “Now then, George, Dr Mackenzie and I just caught a little of your show over there with you mates. We were hoping you could do an encore and tell us a bit more about it.”

“Ah, Mr O’Shea…”

“Paul, George, please… we’re not at work now.”

“Oh... right, of course, Mr… Paul. Well, really, pay no heed to all that. It was just the beer talking and a bit of bravado for the lads, you know,” George flustered.

O'Shea kept eye contact while giving a smile which only reached his cheekbones, "Sounded a bit more than that, George. From the little I caught, it sounded like some critical information about working conditions and the spreading of rumours which could make it difficult to recruit new staff," he crooned, sipping his cider without breaking eye contact.

George reddened, "Mr O'Shea!"

"But I can't imagine a foreman spreading such disinformation. I mean, what would his boss think?"

An awkward silence descended.

"It was noisy though, Paul!" Mackenzie chipped in. Maybe we misheard it, it's possible." She smiled warmly at George, who was now a deeper shade of purple and gazing into the depths of his mild.

O'Shea held the line for a moment longer before shrugging and grinning, "Of course we must have misheard. That's why I asked George over to explain it to us, off the record, didn't I George? I'm sure we'd be interested in hearing it all properly, don't you think Dr Mackenzie?"

"Hayley!"

"Of course, Hayley. Now, why don't I get us three Scotches and you can give us the full story, eh George?" He left George and Hayley together while he went to get the whisky.

Mackenzie gently touched his hand, "It'll be OK, George. He just wants to know what's going on. And it sounds pretty interesting to me, too." George sighed and shook his head.

O'Shea returned with three double malts.

George downed his in one and began. "I'm not comfortable talking about this, Mr O'Shea, 'spcially not in-front of a lady… no disrespect, Dr Mackenzie…"

"Hayley!"

"...Dr Hayley, it's just not summat I'd usually talk of," he mumbled.

"It's OK, George, I'm a big girl!"

"Well, you see," George continued, "It's that place, the one we're lookin' after. I don't suppose as yeh both know the history of the place, do yeh?"

"Well, I know a bit," Mackenzie interrupted.
George nodded, "Of course, Dr Hayley..."

"Just 'Hayley'!"

"Oh yeah, sorry. Mr Bartlett said you wasn't a real doctor! Anyway..." he continued, oblivious to Dr Mackenzie's flushed expression, "I'm talking more as local history and tales. I mean, you might not know that the old lane was knowed as..."

"Yes, we know! And why." Dr Mackenzie assured him.
He nodded and took another sip of his ale.

"Well, you'll know as some of the history what went on there but there are local stories of a Madam Sabrina, who's supposed to haunt the place."

"Oh come on!" protested O'Shea, "You're not telling me that…"

"Wait, Paul!" Mackenzie interjected, " Tell us more about the story. Who was Madam Sabrina?"

George looked towards O'Shea, who nodded. "Well there's sum as says she were a well to do lady and them as says she were a "different" kind of lady if you get my drift." They nodded to show the drift had indeed been got. "Well, legend has it that she murdered a chap, as like her lover or a chap as had slighted her. Course, she were caught an' 'anged but her ghost is supposed to haunt the place, waiting for her chap to come back, I suppose."

"So has this something to do with the lads leaving the job? Are they scared to stay there?" O'Shea asked, only just hiding his incredulity.

“Well, that’s the strange thing, Mr O’Shea. That house ‘as been a lot of things over a lot of years but even quite recently there were a couple of rooms at the top which were rarely used, an’ certainly not slept in.”

“Why not?”

“Well, the usual, knocking noises… I mean like somebody tapping, not the other kind! But people getting strange feelings and such.”

“So, was that happening to your guys?” O’Shea asked.

“That’s the interesting thing, Mr O’Shea, we put some of the younger chaps in there to watch the place, as some of the older ones were a bit wary, believe it or not.”

“Are you wary, George?” Mackenzie asked.

The watchman blushed a little and nodded sheepishly. “Must admit, I am, Ms Hayley but I heard tales from my father, who were a glazier there once. He did a late shift there once and never again!”

“So… a few noises are scaring them, is that it?” O’Shea sighed.

George shook his head. “A bit more than that, strange dreams, erm, strange… sensations! Like they was being touched, a lot, and weird thing was that when they woke, their clothes and things were scattered over the room and their change was missing!”

“What?” Mackenzie and O’Shea chorused.

“Loose change. Gone. Wallet and things scattered. Between that and the… sensations, couldn’t get anyone to stay up there.”

“It couldn’t just be they were drinking a bit and…”

“None of my lads drink, Mr O’Shea, not on the job. We ‘ave our professional pride too!” he stated indignantly.

O’Shea apologized, “But it couldn’t just be someone was coming up while they were asleep and…”

“Locked doors, Mr O’Shea. Not saying it was Madam Sabrina but it were enough to spook ‘em, as it were. It’ll take some work to get any of ‘em to stay there again.”

The production team assembled the following morning. O’Shea was puffing at his vape in solemn thought. As the morning chatter declined, he finally spoke.

“Houston, we have a problem!” The team looked serious, “But, it could be a bit of a godsend!” The team looked puzzled.

O’Shea looked at them all and began quietly, “It seems that some of the security team are scared to stay in the building because of some strange disturbances which they blame on an old legend. Does anyone here know about Madam Sabrina?” One or two local team members raised their hands. O’Shea nodded. “Well, for those who don’t, Dr Mackenzie, here will fill you in. Hayley?”

Mackenzie bade everyone a good morning and opened a file. “OK, as you’re probably all aware, Grope Lane is believed to have been a red light district known, originally as…”

Bartholomew Bartlett opened his mouth to declare but Mackenzie was relentless, “…Gropekuntelane.”

Bartlett sat down in a huff. Some of the team Smiles whilst others tittered quietly.

“Oh titter ye not!” Mackenzie grinned, “It was once a pretty common street name. Anyway, there is a local legend about a ghostly female who is thought to have been one of the local working girls, Madam Sabrina. So the story goes, she killed someone and was executed and now haunts the place.”

Bartlett piped up, “Oh now, now, is this what passes for historical research in your institution? A few old wives’ tales? There is no evidence for this at all...”

“Well actually, Mr Bartlett, there might be. John Frenchman, here has some interesting documentation which he discovered yesterday and I was about to tell Mr O'Shea last night. John?"

John Frenchman coughed and blushed slightly, "Thank you, Dr Mackenzie, Well, it took some finding but there is a rather damaged piece of parchment from the local court records. It seems to be an extraordinary proceeding. It's a bit hard to read, so we've sent it for further analysis, but it mentions a Madame Havren who was found guilty of the murder of a guest in her house. What makes it even more interesting is that she seems to have been hanged from the window of the house itself, rather than the local gallows."

The room was quiet. Bartholomew Bartlett guffawed, "Oh what nonsense, why would anyone be hanged from the window of a house. I'VE never heard of such a thing and I..."

"Presumably as a deterrent to other house-owners doing the same thing. Perhaps the client was somebody important." Frenchman offered.

Bartlett huffed. “But the name is totally different!” he sniped.

Frenchman shrugged, “It appears it could be a Welsh variation of ‘Sabrina’.”

At this, Bartlett rose, slamming the table in frustration, “There is no precedent for such a punishment! It is simply a myth!”

Mackenzie sipped her coffee and savoured her moment, “Perhaps not a precedent, Dr Bartlett, but in August 1530 an Edinburgh tailor was sentenced to be hung from the doorway of his own house for concealing his wife’s death by plague. You can find it in ‘Extracts from the Records of the Burgh of Edinburgh. AD 1528-1557’, published in Edinburgh by the Scottish Burgh Record Society, 1871, page 35!”

Bartlett choked on his cigar.

“So perhaps not as rare a punishment as you assume, Dr Bartlett,” Mackenzie concluded. Bartlett retired to his chair and smouldered.

“So,” O’Shea announced, “we seem to have some historical basis for the legends. This appears to be a significant discovery and so I have discussed with the production company and the site owners, Sunforques, that we extend the episode on the excavations and include a special edition about the local legends and the new information.”

The team chattered excitedly as Dr Bartlett shook his head and gazed into his tea, “The noble discipline of historical research is now brought down to a study of fairy tales!” he sighed.

“Perhaps not, Dr Bartlett. In fact, the ‘fairy tale’ as you call it might be the seed of some new excavations and important discoveries.”

Everybody hushed and looked towards O’Shea.

“You remember, John, what I said early in the project when I asked you to check architectural records?”

"You said something about the lane having been narrowed at some point, I think," Frenchman replied.

"Exactly, and we aren't sure why. Well, I'm just wondering if it was to accommodate something or to help people avoid something."

"Such as?" Bartlett asked, his curiosity rising in spite of himself.

"What normally happened to hanged felons?" O'Shea asked into the air.

"They were sometimes gibbeted or..." Frenchman froze mid-sentence.

"...buried beneath the gallows!" Mackenzie concluded. "Paul, do you think she's down there?"

O'Shea shrugged and grinned, "Which of you would like to find out?"

The evening bells chimed in the local church, a stone's throw from Grope Lane. Paul O'Shea was unpacking his sleeping bag in the upper room of the old house.

Hayley Mackenzie chuckled, "Is your hotel so bad?"

"Well, somebody has to show these big tough security guys that there's nothing to fear and someone needs to be here, so it may as well be me."

"Aw c'mon, we could get some of the diggers to rough it here. They'd be OK with it, I'm sure. Bet they've camped down in worse places," Mackenzie posited.

O'Shea shook his head, "Nope, the buck stops here! Apart from that, it means I don't have to endure Bartlett's moaning over breakfast!" he grimaced.

Mackenzie smirked, "Ah, now I understand! You might like this,

There once was a doctor called Bart,
Who was such an insufferable fart.
He'd slag off your uni,

And make it sound puny,
To make up for his tiny, wee part."

O'Shea burst out laughing at the limerick, "Where's that from?"

"Ah, some of the archaeologist girls were having a drinking competition last night and making up limericks about him."

"Why him, especially?"

"Well, apparently he's been spending a lot of time around the dig, taking photos and such."

"Nothing weird in that is there?"

"Normally, no. But he seems to be very interested in some of the younger diggers, students, the female ones in shorts and t-shirts. They reckon his camera probably has more necklines and thighs than soil and clay."

"Oh god! Has he...?"

“No, they say he’s harmless but annoying. They’ve started wearing longer gear if they know he’s around.”

“Well, as long as he doesn’t start trying to recreate the Lane’s history!”

“I’m sure even Madam Sabrina would think twice!” joked Mackenzie as she left the room.

O’Shea made up his bed on a table and lay down on top of the sleeping bag to read himself to sleep.

The two o’clock chimes sounded and O’Shea felt his eyes partly open. He was aware of the change in room temperature but could not decide if he was awake or not. He tried to move his hand to reach for his phone but seemed to be suffering some form of paralysis. A slight fear began to grow in his mind as he struggled to move.

Then he felt the soft sensation, stroking down his arm.

The feeling moved up his chest and he felt a warmth close to his neck, and gentle touches as if somebody was kissing him. As he tensed his muscles the breathy sigh caressed his ear, "Shhhh!"

O'Shea rolled his eyes to the side but felt something gently push his head back toward the centre, where he was held as if two hands cupped his chin and jaw. A warm, moist breath lightly blew across his throat and face.

The force holding his face slowly moved down his body, pulsating, massaging his chest and moving lower... lower... He realised he was stiffening, rising... and the sensation reached his loins and slipped under the waistband of his shorts.

He felt himself slide out into the open, the warm pulse caressing and massaging his throbbing self.

Suddenly a heavier force seemed to swing over him and pinion him on either side of his ribcage while his arms and chest were stroked and gently pummelled. The weight shifted and his hardened hotness blended with a moist softness as the weight pressed down upon him. He gasped in surprise and ecstasy. The force seemed to close around his lower part and hold it firmly.

O'Shea tried to move his head, to look down his body but once more the "hands" cupped his chin and moved his head backwards before tightening around his throat as the weight rose and lowered rhythmically upon his body. Unconsciously his hips were moving in time to that of the force upon him, his breath quickening and the muscles of his legs and stomach quivering as he resisted, held back... then his hips jerked in a physical crescendo and his being went limp across the table.

Yet the tension around his throat remained. Then it relaxed and he opened his eyes slightly.

Through the crack of his eyelids, he thought he could make out a small, blurred figure rummaging through something, his clothes. A sound of delight and the tightness around his throat eased, Then the weight seemed to dismount. He could breathe easily once more.

A hand stroked his head and face and a smiling visage came close, its breathy warmth on his cheek.

“Thank ‘ee!”

Darkness overcame him.

The sunlight hit O’Shea in the face and he screwed up his face as he woke. He sat up groggily, surveying the scene. His clothes were lying, scattered across the room and his wallet lay disembowelled under a chair. As he sat up he noticed his state of undress and his sex-soiled shorts, from which flopped his flaccid member. Cursing, he tried to rise and clean himself up.

“Morning coffee, Sir!” Mackenzie announced as she threw the door open. “Oooops!”

The hastily dressed O’Shea drained the last of his coffee. He still found it difficult to meet Mackenzie’s eyes.

"So, you think Madam Sabrina came to you in the night?" she asked. He shrugged,

"I don't know! Maybe it's just all the stress and some crazy wet-dream... Damn! I feel like I'm fourteen again and explaining to my mother why I'm washing my sheets!"

"Did you have to explain? I've two of my own and I learned never to ask or comment!"

"Wise! But there's one thing which gets me, my wallet!"

"What about it, is it missing?"

"No, that's the weird thing, my wallet was on the floor, my cards and banknotes were there too but..."

"Your coins had gone?"

"Yep!"

"Maybe Madam Sabrina needed to spend a penny?"

“Or make a phone call?”

“Or maybe paper money and cards didn’t exist in her day but coinage did.”

“I really wish you hadn’t thought of that!”

“Mind you, my real question is...”

“Go on?”

“Was she any good?”

“I really wish you hadn’t asked that!”

The conversation was cut short by a thud outside the door. The thud was followed by a haughty rap at the door, which itself was followed by Bartholomew Bartlett’s head peeping around.

“Ah, just come to check on our brave leader, but I see you are already tending to him!” Bartlett smirked. “Did you have a nice night, Mr O’Shea?”

O'Shea grimaced slightly.

"Ah, it was a bit restless, Dr Bartlett, but thanks for asking. The bells and such, you know!"
"Ah yes, I've heard that things can get a little... hard, sleeping on the table. Especially in this room! Well, I'll see you at the meeting!" With a chuckle, Bartlett disappeared.

Mackenzie and O'Shea looked at each other,

"How much do you think he heard?" Mackenzie asked.

O'Shea shrugged, "Probably most of it but he's likely as not heard the rumours from security too. I wonder what his next move will be?"

"I don't know, but I think our move is to speed up that dig."

O'Shea outlined the plan for the extension of the dig and a new schedule for filming, including interviews of local people, ghost-lorists and historians from the team. He mentioned nothing of the previous evening but made it clear that the rooms were not to be used at night and security would now be based nearer to the excavation area on the ground floor.

“Obviously, we’re moving in new equipment and we don’t want some drunken idiots trying to play Bonekickers!” The archaeologists in the team shuddered at the mention of the defunct TV programme. “Right, if there are no questions, let’s get on with it!” The meeting ended.

“Bart Bart was strangely quiet,” Mackenzie mused, “Do you think he’s plotting something?”

“Maybe! But I don’t see he can do anything detrimental to the project. It wouldn’t be in his interests. Now, I’m off to see George and the guys.”

George met O’Shea’s gaze with a surprising amount of concern. Several other members of the security also nodded to him with an air of sympathy and understanding.

“So now you know, Mr O’Shea!” George said softly.

O’Shea nodded, “Now I know!”

“I’m sorry I didn’t tell you more earlier on, Mr O’Shea, but...”

“It’s OK George, I understand!”

“A bit embarrassing for the younger lads, as you can imagine.”

“Not that much fun for us older ones, eh gents?”

A few serious nods and coughs went around the room.

The following morning the meeting assembled and John Frenchman rushed into the office, his face aglow.

“We’ve got an update on the court record!” he declared. Everyone jumped up excitedly but O’Shea stopped Frenchman from announcing his news.

“It sounds great, John, and I can’t wait to hear it but I think we should wait until Dr Bartlett arrives. Has anyone seen him?”

Nobody had, although some of the archaeologists commented that Dr Bartlett had been seen the previous evening looking rather excited about something but was last seen leaving the Prince Rupert and heading over to Grope Lane, saying he was going to take some night-time pictures.

O’Shea tried Bartlett’s phone but to no avail. After half an hour he shrugged,

“Sod it, if he can’t be here on time he can find out later. Go on, John, let’s hear it!”

Frenchman regained his excitement as he fumbled in his file,

"OK, well it seems we were right. Madam Sabrina was hanged for killing a client. She was the owner of the house and this guy was some local big-shot."

"OK, so we have confirmation. Well done guys! That's fantastic!" O'Shea yelled in glee. Frenchman stopped him with a look,

"There's more! Let me read you a bit," he said, taking a sheet of paper from the file, "Don't worry, we've had it translated into Modern!" he chuckled eagerly.

" And it is hereby decreed by these persons of this court, that the whore and mistress of the said bawdy house is to suffer death by hanging at the hour of noon on this very day. Her accursed corpse having hung from the window of the room wherein she committed her foul deed of murder for one full motion of the sun, shall be laid to rest beneath the steps of that same house as a warning to all who enter and who ply that trade in the locality of Gropekuntelane."

The room was silent. Frenchman looked overjoyed and then the assembly cheered. Mackenzie hugged O'Shea.

"Oh, Paul! We were right! YOU were right! Oh, I wish Bartlett were here to see this!"

Before O'Shea could answer, a solemn security man entered the office. The noise died down when the expression on his face became obvious.

"I think you'd better come upstairs to the rooms, Mr O'Shea!"

O'Shea and Mackenzie reached the top of the stairs, to see another security-man watching the door.

He stepped in front of them, "I think maybe you should look on your own, Mr O'Shea. Sorry, Dr Mackenzie but it's not pretty."

O'Shea opened the door and entered, Mackenzie pushed past the guard and followed. They both stood stupefied. There, across the table, with fierce red lines around his throat, his trousers at his knees and his spent seed upon his stomach, lay the corpse of Dr Bartholomew Bartlett.

The dig resumed after a tasteful few days break. The police had released the body for burial and stated that whilst there were some unexplained aspects of Dr Bartlett's demise, they were not looking for anyone else in connection with it. O'Shea was incredulous.

"A man dies in a room, apparently alone but with red marks around his neck, and they don't think there's anyone else?" he gasped.

His boss shrugged and sipped an espresso, "Well, the autopsy says he died of natural causes, had a heart attack or a stroke, or something."

"I bet he had a stroke! Question is, who was he stroking!?" O'Shea punned darkly. His boss snorted in amusement.

"Himself, apparently! I think the evidence was pretty clear. Seems the excitement was too much for him!"

"But what about the red marks around his neck?"

"You know, Paul, I can't work out why you are trying to delay this project any further," the other man said, shaking his head. "Look, we're in the clear, we've got a great dig, a great subject and now, let's be honest, GREAT PUBLICITY!" he banged the table in crescendo. "And apart from that, nobody seems to know what red marks you are on about, the pathologist didn't see any at all."

O'Shea stared at him. "You're joking! Hayley saw them too, and the security guys. Now you're saying they weren't there when he was on the slab?"

"Apparently so. IF there were any marks, they must have faded. I don't know, I'm not a medical doctor, neither are you. You're a TV producer and you've got something to go and produce, so I suggest you get on with it!"

Mackenzie and O'Shea stood watching the archaeologists.

"I think we're down to a level which corresponds with our time frame," one of the young women called over. "If she's here, it shouldn't be long!"

O'Shea turned and clasped Mackenzie on the shoulder.

She looked back at him with a sad smile on a serious face, "I know, Paul. Let's hope it's worth it?"

"It's just I don't know how I'll react, seeing her!"

"I doubt she looks as good as when you saw her last," she replied drily.

They headed out into the lane and met Frenchman, who was returning from the local Starbucks. O'Shea took his latte and drank deeply. "Just run me through what we have on Madam Sabrina, John."

"Well, this chap she killed was a local merchant, pretty rich and powerful. Madam Sabrina considered him her own personal client and took him upstairs to her private room. Apparently, it was her practice to get them drunk and get a young made to rifle the clothes and purse while she and the client were on the go. According to what we know, he refused to pay her and had no coinage on him. She probably knew her tricks. She was so incensed that she strangled him then and there. The rest, as they say, is history!"

O'Shea nodded and Frenchman went to take the remaining coffees into the office.

"Well, that would explain why all the trousers and wallets got rifled, wouldn't it?" Mackenzie mused. O'Shea stood with his gaze fixed on the black and white house at the corner of Grope Lane.

"Paul, do you think Bartlett deliberately went to...?"

"I'm trying not to entertain the idea, Hayley. Even he..."

"Well, must have been pretty desperate if he did!"

“What you said before, about her not recognising paper money, that’s why she wanted coins,” O’Shea stated flatly.

“Weird, huh?”

“But what would have happened if me, or the lads, hadn’t had any coins? What then?”

“Doesn’t bear thinking about, does it?”

There was a call from the excavation site. A member of the film crew came running over.

“Mr O’Shea, Dr Mackenzie, we think we’ve found her!”

O’Shea threw his empty coffee cup into a nearby bin and they hurried into the site. They were met at the entrance by the dig leader.

“What have we got?” O’Shea demanded

“We’ve just uncovered parts of a skeleton. The skull is intact as far as we can see and there seems to be some damage to the vertebrae in the neck. Obviously, we’ll need to analyze it but it could be consistent with a hanging.”

“Great! Can we see her?” Mackenzie asked. The archaeologist paused. O’Shea’s eyebrows rose in query.

“There’s just something we can’t explain, Mr O’Shea,” she began, “We’ve also uncovered the hand of the skeleton.”

“What’s hard to explain about that?” O’Shea asked, puzzled.

“Well, considering we must be the first people down here in a few centuries and we didn’t reach this level until today... We can’t work out why the skeleton’s hand is holding Dr Bartlett’s credit card.

When the last candle dies…

Trevor Hill

Mamiko felt the hairs on her neck rise as the older girl turned and fixed her with a playful yet malevolent smile. The flames flickered across her face, adding to the demonic glint in her eye. Realising the hold she had over Mamiko, she licked her lips slowly before speaking in a, sing-song voice,

"And the girl, Yuki, went into the toilet… she went to the third door and knocked , 'Hanako San, come out to play!'" As the other girls gasped, Mamiko squealed,

"No, Ayaka, stop… I know about this and it's true…" The group huddled together in the flickering candlelight, as Ayaka continued slowly, sounding each syllable like a drop of water,

"Yes Mamiko, it is true… but you must hear it all… those are the rules!"

Mamiko shuddered. She hated this. One every holiday someone would suggest telling these stupid ghost stories. In the old days, it was called *hyakumonogatari kaidankai* and there were 100 candles in a dark room and people told ghost stories, extinguishing one candle after each tale until there was only one left and then, following the final story, it too was extinguished, leaving the audience in total darkness. Sometimes they stopped at ninety-nine because after the last one was put out it was supposed to be possible to call the spirits. There were only four of them here now, but it still gave Mamiko the creeps, and all the others knew it. Ayaka continued,

"... and when Yuki called, a little voice said, 'I am here...' As she opened the door, Yuki saw a smiling little girl in a pretty red skirt..."

"Sometimes she wears white!" a third girl, Keiko, chipped in, only to be hushed into silence by the single boy in the company.

"Shhhh! Let her finish!" he snapped. Ayaka continued without breaking rythym,

"slowly Yuki opened the door... 'Are you Hanako-San?' she asked. The little girl turned and smiled'Yes, I am...'" The girls gasped at the revelation. Looking at each of them slowly, Ayaka smiled, showing her teeth in the yellow- dance of the flame, before continuing,

"Yuki wanted to scream... the little girl's eyes were blood red... (more gasps from the audience) She tried to turn and run, but Hanako-san grabbed her tightly and said, 'No, you can't go… you called me… now you have to play with me… Forever!' and she pulled Yuki down into the toilet… and when her friends came, all they found was Yuki's handkerchief… covered in… BLOOD!" she concluded, blowing out the candle in her hand to a shriek from the girls and a loud laugh from the boy. The trembling girls began to calm down as the boy, holding the last remaining candle, said,

"That was good, but do you know the story of Aka Manto?"

"No!" choired the girls (except Mamiko), "Tell us, Goichi!" Mamiko clenched her teeth… one more story and then they could put the lights on… but she knew Goichi would drag this one out, just for her.

Goichi smiled at them, the shadows dancing across his face. He paused a second before letting his face go blank, betraying no emotion. Then he began,

"Aka Manto is a charming man, who wears a mask and a red cloak…"

"But who is he?" Ayaka asked.

"Nobody knows," Goichi replied, "but he has the name Aka Manto… 'Red Coat', because of the red coat he always wears… along with his silver mask, so nobody sees his face, which is said to be… horrible…"

"What does he do?" Mamiko squeaked, knowing she would wish she hadn't asked. The boy continued,

"Well, one day a girl went to the toilets in her school, it was an old building…"

"Why do all these ghosts live in toilets?" Mamiko moaned, whose legs had already been crossed for some time.

"So when they scare you, you are in the right place to pee your pants." Keiko replied.

"Quiet!" Ayaka hissed, "Let him tell the story."

"I don't want to hear it if it's too scary," Mamiko whimpered, "I'm almost peeing my pants now!"

"Are you going to let me continue?" Goichi sighed,

"Go on…" Keiko nodded. Taking a breath and resuming his former composure, Goichi went on,

"Well, the girl was looking in the mirror and she heard a handsome man's voice say, 'You look very beautiful, would you like a red scarf… or a blue one?' Without thinking, she said she'd like a red one… and they found her… dead." The girls gasped once more. Mousily, Mamiko enquired,

"But how do they know she asked for a red one if she was dead?"

"Because," Goichi whispered, " her throat was cut open so wide, that all the blood looked like a red scarf. That is what Aka Manto does… that is how they know."

"It's not true!... is it?" Mamiko demanded, pleadingly. Ayaka put a hand on her shoulder and nodded,

"It is, it happened at my cousin's school as well… I heard about it!" she confirmed. Mamiko's eyes widened. Keiko snorted scornfully,

"But it's easy, don't ask for a red scarf… what else can he do?" Goichi smiled knowingly, shaking his head,

"That's not a good idea either," he cautioned, "Another girl heard about Aka Manto and thought the same thing… she went to the toilets and she also heard a voice asking, 'Would you like the red scarf or the blue one?'"

"What did she do?" asked Ayaka.

"Well, the police say she must have asked for the blue scarf… because when they found her…" Goichi said, suddenly standing up with his arm above his head and his head on one side, “she was hanging by a scarf… and her face was blue!” He blew out the candle. The girls screamed satisfyingly. In the darkeness, Mamiko felt a cold shudder go down her back. After a second, Ayaka went to turn the lights on.

“Oh man, that’s weird…” murmed Keiko, “Is it true?” Pleased with his triumphant ending, Goichi sat down.

“Yeah, he’s never been caught… and he’s been seen all round the country.”

“Stop it,” groaned Mamiko, “I’m scared… and I need the toilet.” Chuckling, Goichi rose from his seat and moved out of the circle,

“Do you want something to drink? I’m going to the kitchen…” he declared, walking out before anyone had time to answer.

“In a minute… I really do need to pee…” moaned Mamiko. Ayaka laughed tauntingly,

“Haha! Those stories really scared you, didn’t they?” Mamiko shook her head defiantly,

“NO! I just had too much Coke… do you want to go with me?” she asked. Ayaka and Keiko shrieked with laughter, taunting her together,

“Ha, you are scared… ooooh, scaredy cat!”Mamiko clamped her jaw and shook her head angrily.

“No I’m not…” She snorted, stamping a foot, “ I’ll go alone then, see if I care…” and she stormed out of the room, trying to convince herself as much as the two older girls, who stood watching for a second before spluttering out into fits of giggles. Eventually Ayaka pulled Keiko towards the kitchen,

“Come on, let’s fix something to eat”.

*

Mamiko sneaked down the corridor of the hostel. This was always the other worst part of these school holidays, staying in these creepy old buildings with faulty lighting. They made you believe the stories… Eventually she reached the communal bathroom. Slowly, gingerly, Mamiko pushed the door open. There was a toilet next to a shower cubicle and a wall sink with a mirror. Mamiko fumbled for the light switch, waiting in dread to feel something grab her hand. Finding the cord, she pulled it and checked the bathroom once again… Her reason for coming was getting more pressing and she was less worried about ghosts than the amount of Coke she’d drunk. Scanning the room once more, she went to the sink and splashed some water on her face as if to give herself some courage. Suddenly she thought she saw a movement behind her in the mirror. She snapped her head around but saw nothing, just the slight motion of the shower curtain as the breeze from the window caressed it. Angrily, she scolded her reflection,

"You're so stupid… there's nothing to be scared of… it's just a game and there's nothing real… grow up… or you *will* wet yourself!" Half believing her new courage, she moved to the toilet and, checking once more, slipped her shorts and panties down to her knees before sitting down.

As she began to relieve herself, a deep, male voice crooned softly from behind the shower,

"You look very beautiful… would you like a red scarf… or a blue one?"

Mamiko stiffened, her shoulders rising and her breath quickening… for a second all she could hear was the beat of her own heart pounding over the dribbling sound in the toilet. From the corner of her eye she could see a red cloak and a silver mask moving slowly from behind the curtain. She tried to speak but produced nothing more than a guttural squeak. Once more the voice crooned,

"Come my dear… I have a lovely… red scarf just for YOU!" at which a cold, wet hand stroked her neck. The coldness shocked her into a reaction and Mamiko let loose a piercing shriek of terror and sprang from the toilet. Shrieking again, she ran, only to trip over her shorts as they fell around her ankles. Screaming and sobbing continuously, she crawled madly towards the door before pulling herself up, one hand madly trying to tug up her shorts, before running, shrieking, down the corridor followed by the wild laughter of the red cloaked man, who held onto the sink whilst doubling up with mirth.

Eventually, still laughing, Goichi removed his mask and staggered backwards, sitting on the toilet as he began to calm himself down,

"Hahaha! Oh god, that was so funny… she really fell for it… whooooo! Aka Manto is coming to get you… silly little cow! Oh I wish I'd seen her face… haha! Whoooooooh! Come out to play…"

After a few minutes, he rose and, still chuckling, moved towards the door. Suddenly, he jerked back, his cloak snagging on something. He pulled on it only to find the cloak being tugged back harder, wrenching him backwards. He tried to jump forward but something seized his legs, whipping them from underneath him so that he fell face forward onto the hard, cold tiles of the floor. Before he could move, a small but heavy object landed forcefully on his back and Goichi felt a cold , wet thing slithering up his neck, under his chin. The little hand clamped his jaw and forced his head backwards.

Unable to speak or move his head, Goichi peered out of the corner of his eye, to see a small white face with dripping wet hair that stank of urine. He smelt the stagnant, dank breath as the face came to rest against his, staring from the corner of its own blood red eye into his tearful one. A second slimy little hand snaked over his face and forced itself between his teeth, slowly beginning to prize his mouth open.

The little faced smiled a malevolent yet playful grin as the sing-song little voice giggled,

“You can’t go… you called me…” Then the demonically strong hands wrenched his mouth open and the upper part of his face backwards. As Goichi felt his jaw joint begin to crack and the corners of his mouth tearing apart, Hanako continued in her giggling song, "… now you have to play with me… FOREVER!"

White Hare

Jessica Oeffler

Standing in a corner
Waiting to be seen
Everything around me
Feels like a dream
I could dio tomorrow
No one would care
Out of the corner of my eye
I spot a white hare
-Follow me quickly-
He seemed to say
When I think about it
I've no reason here to stay
-Follow me through this maze
And happiness you'll find-
Telling myself I can do no wrong
I keep everything inside my mind
-I will take you through, he said,
Your every little dream-
I got so scared, I could not speak,
I didn't dare to scream
I followed into a downward spiral

Round   my vision blackness crept
Through all this, my silence,
I uttered not a peep
Waking cold and all alone
Knowing my days of old were done
When there's nothing left but dones and dust
Never again to see the sun
All through my body I could sense
A feeling, one of sleep,
Into which I sank with thanks

But sank, perhaps too deep

Witch (2)

by Carina Ruiz

The moon broke through the clouds, and the man and a young woman stood there, frozen, waiting for something to happen. They were in the middle of an open field, where the scent of wet wildflowers wafted the air. The young woman made her move first by walking up to the man. Her swagger was brisk; with her head held high and eyes focused like a cat on its prey. The man was surprised when she didn't trip on herself in her thick heeled boots as she glided through the wet field to approach him, He now grew nervous each time she drew closer to him.

"Deal?" she said, her voice enticing as she extended her hand toward him. He hesitated then reached out. They shook hands, one with a firm grip while the other was clammy and shaking a bit.

"Good. What do you need?" she asked.

The man couldn't stop wringing his hands together. His eyes scanned around the open field as if someone was watching him. "I need a spell that can put a curse on multiple people," he whispered.

"And how many are multiple? And what kind of curse?"

"Three. And I don't know, any kind. Anything that'll make them leave me alone."

Her eyes narrowed, but she ignored her doubt because at the end of the day she was getting paid for this.

"I'll have it ready by the next full moon, which is a week from now. What's your mailing address so I can send it to you."

"I'd rather you give it to me in person, the car that I have is a piece of shit and I don't think it'll make the drive here again."

She sighed. She was annoyed by this client the moment he emailed her, but money always called her name. She agreed and asked him where they could meet.

He grabbed a grease-stained napkin from his pocket and a pen. He scribbled down the place and handed it to her. Her eyebrows quirked and she stifled a laugh.

"Ah, Pastor Frank's church. A lot of people say he's batshit crazy."

"Yeah sure, whatever. A week, right? I'll have it in a week?"

"Yes. You'll have your curse in a week. Walk straight to where you came from and you'll head back to your car."

"T-Thank you so much, ma'am."

She rolled her eyes and said, "Don't call me ma'am. Ma'am is for old women. 'Miss' will suffice."

The witch walked back to her tea scented home and inside she saw her familiar sleeping soundly on her large cushioned armchair. She was about to start preparing her client's curse for the unfortunate targets. She never did background checks on her clients because all she cared about was their money going inside her bank account, but something was off about this. His eyelids looked heavy and he was constantly shaking as if he were freezing. The dark circles under his eyes indicated that he hadn't slept in a while and his skin was dulled and had several spots of infection. Overall, he looked like a walking disease.

She opened her drawer and reached for her tablet. The search was simple, and she found that his name was Cain Scaggs and he was a heroin addict.

"Ugh. Even his last name sounds like a disease," grumbled her familiar. He was a handsome fox with a large red bushy tail. Mischievous and cunning, like his owner, they had been together for a long time.

"I need you to do me a favor. Scope him out and tell me what he does regularly."

"From the look of his face and arms, we already know what he does in his spare time, but if it's really what you want, I'll do it."

The witch pulled out her grimoire from under the armchair and opened the page with a bright pink marker on the side. She cast her spell and her familiar turned into a man.

Cold and nude, he was wobbly like a new-born calf. His shoulder-length red hair curtained his face. "Why in the gods' name did you turn me into a human? Everything feels so wrong."

The witch opened an old trunk and began rummaging through it. She managed to find a pair of trousers, shoes, and a simple black shirt as well with a sweater. Her familiar looked at her curiously. She always had the right thing handy; like a dark version of Mary Poppins with her infinite bag filled with odd things. She threw them at him. "Because having a fox wandering around a town is going to look suspicious, plus who knows what animal control will do to you. Put these clothes on and follow him."

Once he was dressed, with the help from the witch, he began to head to the door but stopped when she spoke again. "And Loki…I want to know who these three people are, understood?"

Days had passed and each day she looked inside her cauldron filled with glittered blue water to see Loki's progress. Her familiar was right. Cain usually met his dealer daily to get his score and once he got home, he shot the syringe into his skin. Ironically every night he did, he went to Pastor Frank's church for a DAA meeting. He wanted to be clean, but the drug always got the better of him.

The three people that her client wanted to curse turned out to be his family: his mother, father, and brother, whom he hated the most it seemed. They all wanted what was best for him from what she could tell and already had his things packed to send him off to a rehab center.

The full moon came, and the curse was almost finished. It had everything: three crushed fat roaches, three black spiders, three cicada skins, three horseflies, a cup full of bone meal, a handful of eggshells, and the feather of a vulture. The last ingredient she needed was three strips of alligator skin, but her forest didn't have swamps, only clear lakes. She checked the time.

An hour before she had to meet Cain. She went to the door on the left and knocked on it three times, twisting the doorknob twice before pulling.

Musty humid air greeted her. Spanish moss-covered trees shrouded the swamp as if it were a cage. Chirping crickets and croaking frogs inside their hollow homes welcomed the witch. The sun was setting, casting long shadows. In the distance, some ways along an old boardwalk, an old vine-covered plantation house seemed to float on the murky swamp water. She entered without knocking, knowing they knew who called this home once they would sense her.

Inside, hanging vines hung from the occasional crack. Potted plants stood in every corner of the house. There were a few furnishings scattered about as well with old oiled paintings of landscapes on the chipped painted walls. She walked upstairs. Although the house seemed low on furniture and other essentials, inside the master bedroom, the finest furniture turned it into a boudoir of opulence and glory. Heavy red curtains hung from the window. A lounge chair from Persia sat before the fireplace. A king-sized bed with only the finest Egyptian cotton sheets, comforter and pillowcases took up one side of the chamber. The woman she'd come for sat on a velvet-lined reclining chair; a tea cart set just to her right within easy reach.

The woman flicked her wrist and the teapot started doing its job by brewing itself hot tea.

"I didn't expect to see you here, Selene," said the elder woman with a flat smile. "Whatever the occasion is, you should have let me know beforehand."

"I see that you're still an uptight bitch," the witch said, grinning. She watched as her teacup floated toward her, accepting it when it arrived and taking a sip. Perfect, as always. Madame wore her overly dramatic red robe with its long sleeves curled with fur and sheer long train.

"Language! You know how much I hate when you curse."

"Which is why I still do it to you and only you. Where are the others? Surely the coven would be happy to see me."

"They are all out today. Why have you come here, Selene? You left us, what do you want?"

“I need alligator skin for a client’s curse.”

Madame’s eyes scrutinized her as she flicked her wrist for another cup of tea.

“Honestly, Selene. You’re such wasted talent. You had so much potential and you first wasted it attending a mortal college, and now you give petty handouts to commoners for money. And one of these commoners is trying to expose us because of your greed; do you want another Salem trial? You know where we keep our supply, get it and go.”

“First off, I’m not wasting my talent if it’s making me money. And that commoner’s life had been turned upside down with his fucked-up family, so his followers and the people see him as a crazed lunatic.” She set her empty cup down on a nearby armoire. “Thank you for the tea, as always it was lovely.”

Madame scoffed and waved her away, apparently done with their meeting.

The witch went to the pantry and took a handful of alligator skin before heading back home. A migraine was coming on, setting her teeth on edge.

Once home, she poured the various ingredients into her cauldron and chanted her spell. The liquid bubbled and puffed green and yellow smoke. Good. Just as it should. She grabbed her pliers and reached in carefully. Out of the smoke and bubbles came a perfectly brown dry parchment. She folded it and sealed it inside an envelope.

Retouching her dark lipstick, she went to the door and opened it. This time, it led her inside a church.

Pastor Frank's church.

The church wasn't grand. It was humble and quaint. The blue cushioned pews were filled with addicts. Their meeting was still going. One of them had red hair and a knowing smile. She met Loki's eyes and motioned for them to leave outside of the church.

Pastor Frank who was a guest speaker for the DAA meeting saw the witch as she was leaving his chapel. His entire body broke out in cold sweat. He quaked in fear as the memories flooded into his mind; her gleaming dagger, the worlds that he craved, and his family who left him. The fear he had soon boiled into a rage.

"WITCH!" he yelled, pointing at her. Everyone looked to where he pointed. "That's the witch I was talking about. The witch who put a curse on me and ruined my life. Someone call the police so we can send her to prison for her crimes. May God have mercy on your soul, you Devil worker."

The witch could only smile. Everyone was looking at him like he was a demented old man. She hadn't lied. If he tried to expose her, they would look at him as nothing but a lunatic.

She left, Loki following just behind.

The DAA meeting ended. The addicts started heading out the door, some whispering about the crazy pastor and his rants. Pastor Frank ran outside the church and started yelling about the dangers of witches and witchcraft.

The meeting's attendees couldn't tell who to be more worried about, the witch or Frank. One called 911.

"Hello again, old man," she said, watching him approach.

"You evil, soulless witch. You ruined my life, you know that? My son is dead, my wife is in the arms of a man who's half her age, and my daughter is gone forever."

"I didn't curse you. I gave you a choice to stop that, but you chose not to. Your son is dead because of his addiction, your wife is probably getting a good fuck from whoever she's with now, and your daughter chose to be in a community that makes her happy. The keyword here is ‘choice’, which you had, but chose not to take.”

The blue and red lights flashed into the night. After the police had a short conversation with one of the attendees, the officers went to the pastor. Frank loudly argued to the officers and started to become hysterical. They grabbed the pastor and began to drag him towards their squad car. She could hear him as he pleaded with them to cuff Selene for her crimes of witchcraft.

People were recording with their phones, staring at the commotion. The witch and her familiar ignored them and went inside the chapel again.

Her client had stayed inside while the uproar was going on. He saw the witch and took a step back in fear. “D-Do you, have it?”

“I do. But…” the witch stopped. Loki’s brows furrowed and almost asked her if she was okay. She knew that she shouldn’t even be thinking of this, but she wanted to know the reason. “Why? Why do you want to curse your family? They’re only trying to help you. They want you better, they clearly miss you and want to help you, but you push them away and yet you steal from them all the time to get your fix, why?”

His eyes went wide. "What? You're supposed to be the kind who didn't ask questions! I gave you the money, now give me what I asked for you stupid bitch!"

She knew that this was wrong. Innocent people were going to have an irreversible curse cast on them from their flesh and blood whose soul and mind were consumed by a drug that he chose to do himself. But they had made a deal and like any witch, the deal must be upheld.

"In this envelope is your curse. Write down the names of your victims and then burn it and bury the ashes." She handed the envelope over and he looked at it as if it were a tender newborn babe.

"I don't gotta say anything?" Cain asked.

"No. The incantation has already seeped into the paper. Do you want to know what it'll do?"

"I don't give a fuck what it's gonna do as long as it does its job."

"Your choice," she said softly. Selene and Loki left. Outside, the crowd was breaking up, the addicts were going home.

Back in her tree Loki, who was happily back to his fox form, groomed himself. The witch opened her bank account and saw that her pay had arrived, and her account was nice and fat. Despite that, she felt her stomach in knots. She went to her kitchen and opened several cabinets. She gathered her obsidian sphere, several moonstones, white flower petals, salt, and her dagger.

She went outside and drew a circular cleansing sigil on the ground near the shore of her lake. She undressed and dropped the obsidian sphere, the moonstones, the flower petals, and salt in the water. The lake seemed to hum with life and took on a white glow. She stepped into the water and closed her eyes. She allowed her nude body to float and listened to the silence. Her black hair looked like stringy ink that contrasted the glowing white lake.

Loki came out from their hollow home and sat near the shore. He hated seeing his mistress so upset because of one person. She'd done several curses for many of her clients and some of their victims were innocent, why was this one different?

"Why not put a curse on Cain? I bet that will make you feel better." Loki said.

Selene opened her eyes and smiled at the full moon. "Because he already is, Loki. And he just made it doubly worse for himself..."

The fox looked from her up to the starry sky and remembered the evening's events. His addiction was not his only a curse; his family was doomed. Surely, she was right. That was curse enough.

mailto:editor@deeptrax.se

Printed in Poland
by Amazon Fulfillment
Poland Sp. z o.o., Wrocław

52428156R00226